GOOD AS DEAD

Hitch bucked but Fargo was too heavy for him. Hitch speared his fingers at Fargo's neck and Fargo felt the worst pain yet but it didn't slow him or stop him from slamming his fist again and again and again.

Suddenly Fargo realized Hitch wasn't moving. In a daze of pain, he stopped hitting him. Hitch's lips were pulp and his mouth a pool of blood. One cheek resembled mashed meat and one eyebrow was split.

Fargo sank off onto his side. God, he hurt. He managed to sit up and checked Hitch for weapons. All he found was his toothpick, wedged under Hitch's belt. He pressed the tip to Hitch's throat. Hitch's killing days were about over. . . .

THE TRAILSMAN

#357

STAGECOACH SIDEWINDERS

by
Jon Sharpe

A SIGNET BOOK

SIGNET
Published by New American Library, a division of
Penguin Group (USA) Inc., 375 Hudson Street,
New York, New York 10014, USA
Penguin Group (Canada), 90 Eglinton Avenue East, Suite 700, Toronto,
Ontario M4P 2Y3, Canada (a division of Pearson Penguin Canada Inc.)
Penguin Books Ltd., 80 Strand, London WC2R 0RL, England
Penguin Ireland, 25 St. Stephen's Green, Dublin 2,
Ireland (a division of Penguin Books Ltd.)
Penguin Group (Australia), 250 Camberwell Road, Camberwell, Victoria 3124,
Australia (a division of Pearson Australia Group Pty. Ltd.)
Penguin Books India Pvt. Ltd., 11 Community Centre, Panchsheel Park,
New Delhi - 110 017, India
Penguin Group (NZ), 67 Apollo Drive, Rosedale, Auckland 0632,
New Zealand (a division of Pearson New Zealand Ltd.)
Penguin Books (South Africa) (Pty.) Ltd., 24 Sturdee Avenue,
Rosebank, Johannesburg 2196, South Africa

Penguin Books Ltd., Registered Offices:
80 Strand, London WC2R 0RL, England

First published by Signet, an imprint of New American Library,
a division of Penguin Group (USA) Inc.

First Printing, July 2011
10 9 8 7 6 5 4 3 2 1

The first chapter of this book previously appeared in *Grizzly Fury,* the three hundred
fifty-sixth volume in this series.

The Trailsman

Beginnings . . . they bend the tree and they mark the man. Skye Fargo was born when he was eighteen. Terror was his midwife, vengeance his first cry. Killing spawned Skye Fargo, ruthless, cold-blooded murder. Out of the acrid smoke of gunpowder still hanging in the air, he rose, cried out a promise never forgotten.

The Trailsman they began to call him all across the West: searcher, scout, hunter, the man who could see where others only looked, his skills for hire but not his soul, the man who lived each day to the fullest, yet trailed each tomorrow. Skye Fargo, the Trailsman, the seeker who could take the wildness of a land and the wanting of a woman and make them his own.

Colorado, 1860—
caught between a rock and a hard place,
Fargo's going to carve out a new trail—with lead.

1

A shot cracked sharp and clear from around the next bend in the winding mountain road.

Skye Fargo drew rein and placed his hand on the Colt at his hip. A big man, broad of shoulder and chest, he wore buckskins and a white hat turned brown by the dust of his travels. He heard shouts and the sounds of the stage that was up ahead of him come to a stop. Slicking his six-shooter, he gigged the Ovaro to the bend. He could see without being seen.

Four masked men were pointing six-shooters at the stage. A fifth had dismounted. The driver's arms were in the air and the pale faces of passengers peered out the windows.

The fifth bandit swaggered over and opened the stage door.

"Get your asses out here," he barked, "and keep your hands where I can see 'em."

The first to emerge was a terrified man in a suit and bowler. He cowed against the coach and fearfully glanced at the outlaws and their guns.

The next was a woman who had to be in her eighties if not older. She held her head defiantly high and when the outlaw took hold of her arm, she shrugged free and said, "Don't touch me, you filth."

The outlaw hit her. He backhanded her across the face and when she fell against the coach, he laughed.

"Leave her be, damn you!"

Out of the stage flew a young tigress with blazing red hair. She shoved the outlaw so hard that he tottered back, and then she put her arm around the older woman to comfort her.

The outlaw swore and raised his pistol to strike her.

"No," said a man who wore a flat-crowned black hat and a black duster. "Not her or the old one."

1

The man on the ground glanced up, swore some more, and lowered his revolver. "Hand over your valuables," he commanded, "and be quick about it."

Fargo had witnessed enough. He didn't like the odds but he couldn't sit there and do nothing. Staying in shadow at the edge of the road, he rode toward them at a walk. His intent was to get as close as he could before he let lead fly but he was still twenty yards out when one of the robbers pointed and hollered, "Someone's comin'!"

Fargo fired. His shot caught the shouter high on the shoulder and twisted the man in his saddle. Two others started to rein around to get out of there but the man in the black duster and the outlaw on the ground had more grit; they shot back. A leaden bee buzzed Fargo's ear. The man in the duster fired again and Fargo felt a sharp pain in his right leg at the same instant that he put a slug into the outlaw standing by the stage. The man staggered, then recovered and ran to his horse and swung up. Fargo fired yet again but by now all the outlaws were racing up the road. He didn't go after them. He was bleeding.

The driver jerked up a shotgun but the gang was out of range.

Fargo came to a stop next to the stage.

"Don't let them get away!" the terrified man bawled.

Dismounting, Fargo kept his weight on his left leg and hiked at his right pant leg.

"They wing you, mister?" the driver asked.

Fargo grunted and eased down. He pulled his pant leg to his knee. The slug had torn through the flesh of his calf and gone out the other side. "Son of a bitch." Thankfully, though, his bone had been spared. The blood was already slowing.

"Why are you sitting there?" the terrified man demanded. "You should go after them."

"Shut the hell up, Horace," the driver said. "Can't you see he's been shot?"

"Don't you dare talk to me in that tone, Rafer Barnes," Horace said. "I won't have it, you hear?"

Fargo pried at the knot in his bandanna.

A dress rustled and perfume wreathed him. The redhead

smiled warmly and said, "Thank you, sir, for coming to our rescue."

"Let me see that leg, young man," the older woman said, sinking to her knees. "I've tended my share of bullet wounds in my time."

"I've been hurt worse," Fargo said, and went to tie his bandanna over the holes. To his surprise and amusement, she slapped his hand.

"Let me see it, I said." She bent and probed and announced, "It's not serious but you'll be limping for a good long while. I advise you to see a sawbones, though, to clean it up."

"Listen to my grandma," the redhead said. "She always knows what she's talking about."

Fargo wrapped his bandanna and tied it. Without being asked, the young woman slipped an arm under his to help him stand.

"There you go." Her green eyes were luminous in the light of the full moon and her lips were as red as ripe strawberries.

Fargo breathed in the scent of her hair. "I'm obliged, ma'am."

"My name is Melissa. Melissa Hart. This is my grandmother Edna."

The older woman had risen and was brushing off her dress. "How do you do?"

Rafer Barnes leaned down from the seat. "I'm obliged, too, mister, for the help. I'm not supposed to let you, but how about if you ride up here with me the rest of the way and spare your leg?" He paused. "You're bound for Oro City, I take it?"

Fargo admitted that he was and accepted the offer. His wound was less likely to take to bleeding again than if he rode the Ovaro. He tied the stallion to the back of the coach, limped to the front, and climbed on. The women and Horace were already inside.

Rafer offered his hand. "Those owlhoots would have done us harm if you hadn't come along when you did."

Fargo didn't mention that he had been behind the stage most of the way from Denver. "They'd have robbed you and gone their way." That was how most stage robberies went.

3

"No, sir," Rafer said with an emphatic shake of his stubble. "They'd've shot Horace and me and beat on the ladies as a warnin'."

"What makes you so sure?"

Rafer lashed the team. Under them the stage creaked and rattled. When the horses were in motion he said, "I reckon you haven't heard about the war."

"The what?"

"The *Oro Gazette* is callin' it the Stagecoach War. The company I work for and another are out to be top dog in Oro City and the squabble has become downright vicious."

Fargo had noticed the name of the line when he climbed up. "I've heard of the Colorado Stage Company. What's the name of the other?"

"The Cobb and Whitten Express. It's named after the two gents who own it. Cobb I don't know much about but I've met Whitten and he can be a pushy gent. I reckon he doesn't like competition."

"There's not enough business for two stage lines?" Fargo recollected hearing that a gold strike gave birth to Oro City about a year ago.

"More than enough. The Denver run brings in a heap of money and there are other runs to other towns and mining camps and settlements."

Fargo sat back. His leg was bothering him and he'd like to spend the rest of the ride quiet but Rafer was a talker.

"Yes, sir. Oro City is growin' by leaps. Give it a couple of years and it'll be almost as big as Denver."

Fargo had his doubts. He'd heard that most of the gold was placer with a lot of sand mixed in.

"We've already got nearly as many saloons," Rafer related. "For lendin' a hand back there, I'll treat you to a drink when we get to town."

"Make it a bottle."

Rafer laughed. "I reckon that's fair." He glanced at Fargo. "I should warn you, though. You hit two of them. They're liable to want to get even."

"Do me a favor and keep quiet about it."

"Fine by me but you're forgettin' the folks in the stage. They'll gab. The *Gazette* will hear of it and by tomorrow night everyone in Oro City will know who you are and what you did."

"Hell."

"Sometimes it doesn't pay to be one of those—" Rafer stopped. "What do they call 'em? Good Samaritans?"

The stage lurched up a switchback and Rafer devoted his attention to handling the ribbons. "Easy there," he said to the horses as the wheels rolled dangerously near the edge.

Fargo glanced down. He wasn't bothered by heights but the five-hundred-foot drop to jagged boulders was enough to make anyone's skin crawl.

"Don't worry. We won't go over," Rafer said, and chuckled. "I've been handlin' a stage for more years than you've been alive."

"Is that a fact?" Fargo said, still staring over the side.

"It sure enough is. I got my start as a cub on a Boston line years ago and then came west. Been out here ever since." Rafer guided the team around a sharp turn with the skill born of the long experience he claimed. "How about you? What do you do for a livin'?"

"This and that."

"You don't care for me to pry? Fair enough. But if I was to guess I'd say you make your livin' as a scout."

"My buckskins give me away?"

Rafer grinned. "Lots of people wear deer hides. Hunters, trappers, you name it." He shook his head. "No, I'd peg you for a scout because you have that look scouts have."

"I have a look?"

"Take a gander in a mirror sometime," Rafer said. "It's those hawk's eyes of yours. Like you're lookin' far off when the rest of us can only see up close."

"That makes no sense."

"It does if you're a pigeon and not a hawk," Rafer said, and cackled.

Fargo folded his arms and made himself as comfortable as he could. The wind was chill at that altitude at night even in the summer. Overhead, stars sparkled. To the south a coyote serenaded them.

Rafer breathed in deep and exclaimed, "God Almighty, I love this country."

Fargo shared the sentiment. The mountains and the prairie were as much a part of him as his arms and his legs. He could no more do without the wild places than he could do without women.

"Did you see that?" Rafer asked.

Fargo looked up. They were climbing toward the crest of a ridge. As near as he could tell, the stretch of road to the top was clear. "See what?"

"Up yonder," Rafer said, and pointed at the top. "I saw somethin' move."

"A deer, maybe," Fargo said. Or it could have been an elk or a bear or another animal.

"No. I thought I saw the shine of metal. Maybe . . ." Rafer got no further.

The night was shattered by the thunder of rifles. Lead struck the coach with loud *thwacks* and one of the horses whinnied.

Fargo's Henry was in his saddle scabbard. He clawed at his Colt even though the range was too great. "Do you have a rifle?"

Instead of answering, Rafer dropped the ribbons and cried, "I'm hit!"

2

The team exploded into motion. Since the road was too narrow for them to turn around and walls of vegetation hemmed it, they had only one direction to go—up the grade toward the outlaws.

Drawing his Colt, Fargo extended his arm and took as deliberate aim as he could with the coach swaying and bouncing, and squeezed off a shot at a silhouette on horseback. He was rewarded with a cry. He fired again and he must have come close because one of them shouted in alarm and they reined their mounts around and fanned the breeze.

Rafer was slumped over, a hand pressed to his shoulder. "The team!" he shouted.

Fargo snagged the ribbons. He hauled on them and the stagecoach clattered over the crest and came to a stop.

"What's going on up there?" Horace yelled.

Fargo commenced to reload. "How bad is it?" he asked without taking his eyes off the road and the woods.

"Let's find out," Rafer said, sitting up. He slid his hand under his shirt and after a bit uttered a bleat of grateful surprise. "They nicked my collarbone."

"Lucky," Fargo said. He finished reloading and twirled the Colt into his holster. Gripping the rail, he swung down. His leg protested as he limped around the stage to the Ovaro and yanked the Henry clear of the scabbard.

Horace poked his head out. "What was all that shooting about?"

Ignoring him, Fargo opened the door. "Are you ladies all right?"

"I asked you a question," Horace said.

"We're shaken up but otherwise we're fine," Melissa said.

7

She had her arm over Edna's shoulders.

"Answer me, consarn you," Horace said.

"Until we get to Oro City you should sit on the floor," Fargo suggested.

"On the floor?" Horace said. "It's too cramped."

"Better than being dead." Fargo went to close the door but Horace pushed against it with his foot.

"Hold on. You still haven't answered me. What were you shooting at up there?"

"Mosquitoes." Fargo shoved Horace's leg and slammed the door.

"Do you honestly expect me to believe that?"

"Jackass." Fargo limped to the front and reclaimed his perch on the seat.

Rafer had unbuttoned his shirt to examine his right shoulder. He was still bleeding but only a trickle. "I'll have another scar to add to my collection," he said, and chuckled.

"You're taking this awful well."

"I've been shot before." Rafer touched thick scar tissue on his ribs. "This one was a drunk who didn't like me sayin' he was as dumb as a tree stump." He put his finger to another scar on his other side. "This one, I was in a saloon when two gents took to squabblin' over cards. When the shootin' started I dived for the floor but I wasn't quick enough." He gingerly pulled his shirt back on. "How about you, friend?"

"I've got my share," Fargo said. He didn't elaborate.

Rafer tried to move his arm, and winced. "I can't hardly move it." He frowned. "I don't suppose you've ever handled a stage?"

"Once or twice."

"Then I'd be obliged if you would take us in. It's against the rules but the rules be damned."

Fargo had no objection. He got under way, shouting down for the benefit of the ladies, "Stay low like I told you."

"You're thinkin' those sons of bitches will try again?" Rafer said.

Fargo shrugged. "Tell me more about this stage war."

"I'm just a driver. I don't know all the particulars beyond what I've already told you. If you want to learn more, you need to talk to the gal I work for."

"Gal?" Fargo said.

"Brandy Randall is her handle. The Brandy is short for Brandywine. Her husband started the Colorado Stage Company but he went and died of a stroke about a year ago and she's been runnin' it by her lonesome ever since. Does a damn good job, too."

"Is the other line bigger?"

"I'll say. The Cobb and Whitten Express has more of everything. More stages. More horses. More drivers. More shotgun messengers. But that's not enough for Whitten. You ask me, he aims to take over the whole territory by driving all the smaller stage lines out of business."

Fargo had met men like Whitten before. They hankered to be top dog, and to hell with anyone who stood in their way. "How many stage robberies have there been?"

"Tonight makes four," Rafer said. "But this time they didn't get anything thanks to you."

"Did you recognize any of them?"

Rafer opened his mouth, hesitated, and closed it again. "No."

"You'd make a terrible poker player," Fargo said.

"I'm not admittin' nothin'," Rafer said. "But let's say you're right and maybe I did—it wouldn't be healthy for me to say."

"You're scared."

Rafer nodded. "Damn right I am. I'm fond of breathin'. And if one of those owlhoots was who I think it was, he's snake mean and lightning fast. If he hears I'm accusin' him of bein' a stage robber, he'd hunt me down and blow out my wick."

"How about having the law protect you?"

Rafer snorted. "Mister, I wouldn't trust Marshal Shicklin as far as I can throw this coach."

"Why not?"

"I've already said too much. You want more answers, talk to Brandy."

"I might just do that," Fargo said. He never had been one to forgive and forget. He'd like to find out who put the slug in his leg and return the favor.

The rest of the ride Rafer was quiet.

Fargo had his hands full with the stage. His leg stopped

throbbing but it hurt like hell and was stiffening when they eventually crested the last height.

Oro City spread out before them. As with most boom settlements, calling it a city was putting the cart ahead of the horse. The streets were dirt and dust, the buildings a mix of frame houses and stores with false fronts, plus cabins and tents and lean-tos. The promise of riches had brought a horde of gold seekers and those who preyed on their pokes and their vices. Saloons outnumbered all the other businesses combined, and for every two liquor mills there was a brothel.

The tinny notes of a badly played piano tinkled on the air. Gay laughter filtered past batwings and the hubbub of voices was constant.

Fargo drank it all in. He hankered for a game of cards, a bottle of whiskey, and a willing dove, not necessarily in that order. But he had his wound to think of.

Fargo slowed as a precaution and yelled at a pair of drunks who were singing so loud they didn't hear the stage.

The Colorado Stage Company had a small office. To one side were a corral and a stable.

Fargo was bringing the stage to a stop when the door opened and out stepped a woman. She was in the dark shadow of the overhang and he didn't see her clearly until she stepped into moonlight. Right away his interest was kindled.

She was tall and slim with legs that went on forever. Instead of a dress, she wore a man's shirt and britches and boots. Her long brown hair was tied at the back with a pink ribbon and hung in a tail across her neck and down her front to her ample bosom. In another unladylike gesture, she wore work gloves and had a revolver strapped to her waist. After lighting a lamp that hung on a peg, she turned with a smile that quickly died. "Rafer? Why is that—" She stopped and in a lithe bound was at the stage. Pulling herself up, she anxiously asked, "Is that blood on you? Tell me what happened."

"Another try at us, Brandy," Rafer said. "Me and this hombre were both hit. We could use the doc."

Brandy's green eyes fixed on Fargo and his leg. Without another word she was off the stage and ran inside. She yelled something and within moments a boy of fifteen or so bolted out jamming a battered straw skimmer on his head and sprinted off down the street.

Fargo climbed down and propped the Henry under him as a crutch.

Brandy reemerged and was about to clamber to the seat when Horace stuck his head from the window.

"I say, madam. I am afraid I must protest the quality of your service."

"What?"

"As a paying passenger I expect better treatment."

"You do, do you?"

Horace nodded and recited a litany of complaints. "We were an hour late leaving Denver. The ride was atrocious. Just when I thought it couldn't possibly get any worse, we were nearly killed by highwaymen and then had to sit on the floor the rest of the way here. Now we're ignored and left to fend for ourselves."

"You look to be a grown man."

"What does that have to do with it? Do you or don't you serve the public?" Horace sniffed. "I demand that you treat me as I deserve."

"Good idea," Brandy said. She opened the door and pulled down the step. "Here you go."

"Thank you, my dear."

Brandy smiled sweetly and reached up and grabbed him by the front of his shirt with both hands.

"What in the world are you doing?" Horace squawked.

"Helping you down," Brandy said, and with impressive strength, she hauled him out and sent him tumbling to the ground.

Rafer laughed.

Horace sat up and looked down at himself in amazement. "How dare you?"

Brandy put her hands on her hips. "On your way, little boy."

Brushing at his suit, Horace stood and glared. "You're lucky I didn't break a bone. I have half a mind to report you to the marshal."

"You've got that much right," Brandy said.

"That I should report you?"

11

"That you have half a mind."

Rafer laughed louder, which made Horace madder. Balling his bony fists, he shook one at Brandy. "You think you're so smart. I'm going straight to the marshal and have you arrested for assault."

"No," Fargo said. "You're not."

Horace looked at him in some surprise. "What did you just say?"

"You heard me." Fargo moved closer. He was a foot and a half taller and towered over the mousey malcontent. "Make yourself scarce."

"Who do you think you are?" Horace demanded. "You can't go around threatening people."

Fargo put the Henry's muzzle to the tip of Horace's nose. "How stupid are you?"

The next moment a barrel-chested man with a tin star pinned to a brown leather vest strode into the ring of lantern light. On his right hip was a Remington revolver.

"What the hell is going on here?"

3

Horace darted to the lawman's side and pointed an accusing finger at Fargo. "You're just in time, Marshal Shicklin. Arrest that man. He was about to shoot me."

"Shut up, Horace," the lawman said. "I'll get to you in a minute." He was staring at Brandy Randall. "That boy who works for you was flyin' down Main Street and I stopped him and asked why. He said two people have been shot and he had to get the doc."

Brandy nodded at Fargo and then at Rafer. "This stranger and my driver."

"It was the stage robbers," Rafer said. "Or they were pretendin' to be."

"How do you pretend to rob a stage?" Shicklin said.

"Damn it, Oren," Brandy snapped at him. "When are you going to do your job and arrest Cobb and Whitten?"

"We've been all through this," the lawman said in mild exasperation. "Do you have proof Cobb and Whitten are behind these holdups?"

"They're too smart for that. But we both know it has to be them."

"Do we? You seem to forget that their stages have been hit, too."

"They do that so no one will suspect."

"Again, I need proof." Marshal Shicklin turned to the rest of them. "Did you get a good look at the robbers, Rafer? Any of them you recognized?"

"It was dark and they were masked."

"So I have nothing to go on, like always."

"Arrest Cobb and Whitten and the robberies will stop," Brandy said.

Marshal Shicklin sighed. He looked Fargo up and down and said, "Who might you be?"

Fargo told him.

"Anything you can add? Did you get a better look than Rafer?"

Fargo gave a short account, ending with, "I hit a couple of them."

"You don't say? Then they'll need doctoring. I'll nose around and see what I can find out."

"Which will be nothing," Brandy said.

The lawman turned to go but Horace blocked his way.

"Aren't you forgetting about me?"

"I'm trying to."

Horace again jabbed his bony finger at Fargo. "I want him arrested. He was going to shoot me."

"Is that true, mister?"

"I wouldn't waste the bullet," Fargo said.

The lawman chuckled and said, "Run along, Horace."

Horace did no such thing. He grabbed the marshal's arm and demanded, "Who are you going to believe? Some buckskin-clad bumpkin or a pillar of our community?"

"Pillar of our community?" Marshal Shicklin repeated, and laughed. "Horace, you run a dry goods store, for God's sake."

"Now you hold on," Horace said. "I won't be demeaned in public."

"Then don't open your mouth." Marshal Shicklin knocked Horace's hand away. "It's been a long day. I'm tired and I need a drink. So I'm going to forget you put your hand on me. But if you ever do it again I'll break your goddamn arm." Horace opened his mouth to speak but the lawman raised a finger. "Not another word. Go to your store and your old lady or I'll arrest you for being a nuisance."

"I never," Horace said indignantly. Wheeling, he marched off with his skinny back as stiff as a board.

"The jackasses I have to put up with," Marshal Shicklin said. He touched his hat brim to Brandy. "I'm sorry you think so poorly of me. I do the best job I can."

"Which isn't saying much," Brandy said.

The lawman departed.

"Kind of hard on him, weren't you?" Fargo asked.

"He's useless," Brandy declared, "and I'm sick and tired of having my stages stopped and my passengers and hired help terrorized."

Rafer was climbing down and grumbling to himself. He could only use one hand and slipped and almost fell. Brandy helped him the rest of the way.

Fargo licked his dry lips. The lawman wasn't the only one who could use a drink. He was about to say to hell with waiting for the doctor and go find a saloon when the boy Brandy had sent off returned with a portly man wearing spectacles and carrying a black bag.

"Here's the sawbones," the boy announced.

"I'm obliged, Jimmy," Brandy said. "And I'm obliged to you, Doc Jolsen, for coming so quick."

"It's what I do, after all," the doctor said absently while appraising both Fargo and Rafer. "Hmmm. One in the leg and the other in the shoulder. Do you need help getting to my office or can you make it on your own?"

"Lead on, Doc," Rafer said.

"You can't tend them here?" Brandy asked.

"My dear woman," Doc Jolsen said. "I will have to probe and clean and perhaps perform surgery. The more sanitary the conditions, the better for my patients." He beckoned and walked off without waiting for them to follow.

Fargo saw Melissa peering out of the stage; he'd forgotten about her and her grandmother. Neither had let out a peep while the marshal was there, and they seemed to be waiting for everyone else to leave. He thought that was peculiar but it was none of his business so he limped after the physician.

Rafer caught up to him and said, "This is a hell of a note."

"Do you want infection to set in?" Fargo knew of men who lost arms or legs or died from even small wounds.

"I meant bein' shot. If I had any brains I'd quit and go work for someone else. But I won't run out on Brandy when her back is to the wall."

"She's easy on the eyes, too."

"Don't even think it," Rafer said. "A lot of horny toads have tried. She always plants her boot on their backside. She is all business, that gal."

15

Boomtowns were beehives of bustle and Oro City was no exception. The streets were thronged with townsmen and prospectors, gamblers and ladies in too-tight dresses sashaying their wares, and those with the predatory stares of wolves.

Doc Jolsen's office was on the second floor of a feed and grain. He huffed as he climbed and groped his pockets to find the key. They waited while he lit a lamp. He had them take chairs while he went into the next room to prepare.

Rafer gingerly rubbed his shoulder. "I don't know about you but I hurt like the dickens."

"Being shot will do that," Fargo said.

"Funny man," Rafer replied. "But we were lucky, the both of us."

Fargo leaned the Henry against the wall, stretched his legs out, and leaned back. His stomach rumbled, reminding him he hadn't had a bite to eat since sunup.

Rafer heard, and chuckled. "Sounds like your ribs are stickin' to your backbone. When we're done here I'll treat you to supper. It's the least I can do after you risked your hide helpin' us."

Fargo had no objection. Afterward, he would indulge his fondness for nightlife. "Which is the best saloon in town?"

"Best how?" Rafer said. "Best whiskey? Best doves? Or the best place to gamble?"

"All three."

Rafer scratched his stubble. "I reckon you want the Filmore House. The whiskey ain't watered down, the doves are right pretty, and the games ain't crooked, or so folks say. It's down the street about two blocks."

"Go there a lot?"

"Me?" Rafer said, and laughed. "Not on the money I make. Or didn't I mention it's the most expensive proposition this side of anywhere?"

The sawbones emerged and bid Rafer enter. Fargo had to wait for close to twenty minutes before Rafer came out again, his shoulder newly bandaged.

"Watch yourself," Rafer warned. "He likes to poke and prod. About made me scream."

"I heard that," Doc Jolsen said. "And I'll have you know I was as gentle as is humanly possible."

16

"So you say, Doc." Rafer smiled at Fargo. "I'll ask Brandy if we can put your stallion up in the company stable and come meet you at the Filmore in about an hour."

"Tell her I can pay for a stall," Fargo offered.

"After what you did?" Rafer shook his head. "I know her like I know my own self. She won't take a cent."

"Shoo," Doc Jolsen said. "You're gabbing when this man has blood all over his leg."

"It's not that bad," Fargo said.

"I'll be the judge of that."

The physician had Fargo strip off his boots and pants and lie on his back on a long table. Beside it was a smaller table with the open black bag and instruments in a row.

Setting a lamp next to Fargo's leg, Doc Jolsen bent and lightly felt the entry and exit wounds. "It could be a lot worse—"

"Told you," Fargo said.

"I wasn't finished." Jolsen selected a probe, carefully inserted the tip into the hole the lead made going in, and pried.

Fargo grit his teeth at a pulse of fresh pain.

"Hmmmmmm," Jolsen said, his left eye practically touching the skin. "How long ago did this happen?"

"About two hours ago," Fargo answered. "Maybe two and a half."

"You should have cleaned it right away." Jolsen selected a long instrument with a short blade at one end. "It doesn't take long for infection to set in. See this discolored flesh? I'll scrape it and cauterize the wound but I can't guarantee I'll get it all."

"Are you saying it might spread?"

"I am saying exactly that, yes. My advice to you is to take it easy for a week to ten days. Avoid anything that might aggravate your leg. No riding, for instance. Don't do a lot of walking if you can help it."

"Hell," Fargo said.

Doc Jolsen reached into his black bag and produced a bottle. "Would you care for some laudanum?"

Fargo had heard of it. Also known as tincture of opium, it was said to kill most any pain. It was also hard to shake once the need was gone. "For a damned bullet hole?"

"Two bullet holes, to be precise," Doc Jolsen said. "A swig now will dull the pain when I start to cut."

"I can take it," Fargo said.

Doc Jolsen grinned. "Suit yourself. But don't say I didn't warn you. Scream if you want. No one will hear except me."

"I won't let out a peep," Fargo predicted.

Once the sawbones inserted the new instrument and commenced to twist it back and forth, it took every ounce of self-control Fargo possessed not to raise the rafters. As it was, when Jolsen finally laid the bloody instrument aside, Fargo was clammy with sweat and felt as if he had just run five miles.

"You're a tough son of a bitch—I will give you that," Doc Jolsen said by way of praise.

"I've never much liked crybabies and I'll be damned if I'll turn into one."

The physician wiped his leg and applied a bandage and stepped back. "You can put your pants on now."

"He doesn't have to on my account," said a female voice from the doorway.

Brandywine Randall was leaning against the jamb.

4

Some men might have clutched at their pants to cover themselves. Not Fargo. He grinned and said, "Like what you see?"

Brandy appraised him as a horse buyer might appraise prime horseflesh. "I've seen worse."

"Miss Randall!" Doc Jolsen exclaimed. "This is private, if you don't mind."

"That's all right, Doc," Brandy said. "He doesn't have anything I haven't seen before."

"Brazen hussy," Doc Jolsen said, but he was smiling when he said it. "Honestly, now. Step outside while he dresses."

"If I have to."

"You do."

Brandy backed out and almost had the door closed when she said, "I'd like to have a word with you, mister, when the doc is done."

Fargo took his time dressing. His leg was throbbing. Each tug on his boot sparked pain. He paid the sawbones and retrieved the Henry and limped into the front room. Brandy wasn't there. He opened the front door. She wasn't anywhere in sight. He stepped outside.

A shadow separated from a black patch in a corner of the porch.

"Here I am."

"Hiding from someone?" Fargo joked.

Brandy came to the rail and gazed up and down the busy street. "As a matter of fact, I am. Didn't Rafer tell you about the goings-on here?"

"About the Stagecoach War?" Fargo nodded. "Where did Rafer get to?"

"I told him to stay at the office and keep an eye on things.

That stage you brought in is the only one in working order. I can't have anything happen to it." Brandy's face clouded. "I'm so desperate, here I am talking to a total stranger."

"I don't savvy," Fargo said.

"Are you hungry?"

"Are you paying?"

"No. But I'll rustle up some grub at my place. It's not far. What do you say?"

Fargo liked her eyes. He also liked the sleek sweep of her thighs, and imagined her long legs wrapped around his waist. "Lead the way, lady."

Brandy opened the doc's gate for him. She matched her pace to his and walked with her hand on her Starr revolver.

"You act like you expect to be shot."

"I do. If Cobb and Whitten kill me, my stage company folds. They've already tried twice."

Fargo was surprised. The murder of a woman nearly always incited public outrage. Guilty parties were invariably treated to a hemp social after a token trial. "How did they try?"

Brandy was scanning the yards and recesses. "The first time a bale of hay fell from the loft in our stable. If I hadn't heard a sound and looked up, it would have crushed my skull." She paused. "Next they tried an arrow. I was in the corral and if I hadn't turned my head, it would have gone clean through."

"An arrow?" Fargo repeated. "Did they think hostiles would be blamed?"

Brandy shrugged. "Maybe they don't care. All I know is I have to watch my back every minute of the day and it gets tiresome after a while." She turned into a path that led through high grass to a small frame house. "Here we are," she said, fishing for a key. "I don't come here much these days. Most of the time I'm at the stage company."

Fargo trailed after her into a parlor. She lit a lamp and bid him make himself comfortable on a settee. He leaned the Henry against it and eased down, glad to take the weight off his leg. The short walk had increased the pain.

"Would you like coffee or something stronger?" Brandy asked.

"As strong as you've got."

She went to a walnut cabinet and returned carrying a whiskey bottle. "Will this do?"

"Monongahela," Fargo read the label. "It will do right fine."

"I'll fetch a glass."

"Don't bother." Fargo took the bottle, opened it, and savored a long swig. Smacking his lips in satisfaction, he grinned and offered it to her.

Brandy shook her head. "Thanks, but I need a clear head. Rest here while I see about something to eat. Would beans and pork suffice?"

"So long as I can have ten helpings."

Fargo leaned back and went on drinking while listening to her putter around in the kitchen. Pots and pans clinked and he heard an oven door squeak. His stomach did more rumbling.

He raised the bottle to his mouth and happened to glance at a window.

A face was peering in at him.

Fargo glimpsed a swarthy complexion and a fierce countenance. An Indian, he thought, or maybe a half-breed. It was there and it was gone. He forgot his leg and heaved up off the settee and nearly fell when his leg buckled. Regaining his balance, he put his hand on his Colt and cautiously moved to the window. The yard was empty. He shuffled back to the settee and eased down.

Brandy was gone a while. The aroma of cooking food filled the house.

Fargo was so hungry his stomach hurt. He'd downed half the bottle when she arrived from the hallway carrying a tray with two plates heaped with beans and slabs of pork and thick slices of buttered bread.

"Would you rather eat here or at the kitchen table?"

Fargo's mouth was watering. "Here is fine." He accepted his plate and placed it on his lap. Breaking a slice of bread in half, he dipped it in the beans, bit off a mouthful, and groaned in ecstasy.

Brandy laughed. "Goodness, a body would think you hadn't eaten in a coon's age."

Fargo was too busy chewing to reply. He ate with keen

relish and when he was done he used the other half of the slice of bread to mop his plate clean. "I'm obliged."

"It's the least I could do after the favor you did me. I almost feel guilty inviting you here to ask another."

Fargo arched an eyebrow.

"Let me take care of our plates and I'll explain."

Leaning back, Fargo had another swallow of whiskey.

A feeling of lassitude came over him and he shook it off. He had something to do. Setting the bottle down, he rose, remembering to put most of his weight on his good leg, and gripped the Henry.

Brandy returned and started toward her chair but stopped. "What are you doing? You're not leaving, I hope."

"Bring a light," Fargo said, and hobbled toward the front door.

"I beg your pardon."

"A lamp or a lantern," Fargo said. He held the door open and when she hurried after him with a lamp in her hand, he headed around the house.

"Do you mind telling me what this is about?"

"You had a visitor while you were cooking supper," Fargo explained. "I saw him at your window."

Brandy blinked. "And you didn't think to tell me until now?"

"He ran off. We weren't in any danger." Fargo came to the window and bent low to study the ground.

"Did you get a good look?"

"I'll know him if I see him again." Fargo added, "He was part Indian."

"He must be the one who shot the arrow at me," Brandy said. "It would be just like Cobb and Whitten to have a half-breed working for them."

There were no prints in the grass under the window. Fargo unfurled and roved toward the fence. In a bare patch of dirt he discovered what he was looking for: a clear track. "He wears moccasins."

"That doesn't tell us much. Most Indians do."

"He weighs about a hundred and fifty. He's short, about five feet to five feet five. And he's part Ute."

"How in the world can you tell that?"

Fargo pointed. "From the cut of the moccasin. No two tribes make theirs alike. He also has a scar on his left cheek and a hooked nose."

Brandy regarded him thoughtfully. "You don't miss much, do you?"

"Not if I want to keep on breathing." Fargo went to the fence but there was nothing more to find. They returned to the house. Brandy threw the bolt, then excused herself and went from window to window, checking that each was latched.

"Now, then," she said as she took her seat, "I've kept you waiting long enough. Let's get to it."

Fargo tried to recollect if he had ever sat in a parlor with a woman wearing a revolver. "I am all ears."

Brandy hesitated. "First off, I'm reluctant to do this, you being hurt, and all. But I'm desperate. All but two of my drivers quit when the violence started and now both of them are hurt." She breathed in deep. "I'd like you to come work for me."

Fargo began to respond but she held up her hand.

"Please. Hear me out before you make up your mind." Brandy gazed out the window. "It's been pure hell for me these past few months. Cobb and Whitten have done all they can to drive me out of business and they've damn near succeeded. They've ruined most of my stages. They've driven off most of my help. I'm hanging on by a thread." She tiredly rubbed her eyes. "I've tried to hire new help but no one wants to risk being crippled, or worse. Rafer and Jimmy and my other driver, Frank, have stayed on, but now Rafer has been shot and the doc says he shouldn't handle a team for a week or so and Frank has a busted foot and is on crutches and Jimmy, well, he's just a kid."

Fargo knew what she was leading up to and let her get to it in her own sweet time.

"I have to keep operating to stay in business. If I don't, I'm done. I can take some of the runs myself but I need someone to take the others." Brandy fixed those penetrating eyes of hers on him in earnest appeal. "You can handle a team. You proved that by bringing the stage in. And you don't scare easy. You proved that by driving those polecats off. I know

23

you're hurt. I heard the doc say you have to go easy on your leg. But you can still handle a stage. And I'll pay double the going rate if you'll agree to work for me." She smiled thinly. "Who knows? You might come to like it and stay on."

"No," Fargo said.

Brandy's face fell.

"I couldn't do it permanent," Fargo said. He liked the wide open spaces too much, the mountains and the prairies that were as much a home to him as this house was to her. He liked being able to go wherever the wind blew him. "But I'll help you for a week or two." By then his leg would be healed enough that he could be on his way.

"That's something, anyway," Brandy said, sounding disappointed.

"It's more than that."

"How do you mean?"

"Rafer thinks that the men who shot me were working for Cobb and Whitten."

"That would be my guess, yes."

"Then Cobb and Whitten have a lot to answer for," Fargo said. "And before I'm done, they sure as hell will."

5

The Filmore House was everything Rafer claimed. A glittering chandelier sparkled like diamonds, the tables were covered in felt, and gleaming brass spittoons were ranged along the bar. Tiers of shelves held every liquor there was. The bartenders wore jackets and aprons. The doves wore dresses fancy enough for New York or New Orleans.

Fargo limped in through the batwings. Glances were cast at the Henry and then at his leg. He made his way to the bar and stood with his back to it, surveying the room. Poker, keno, and blackjack were the games of choice. A roulette wheel was being spun. He breathed in the whiskey and tobacco smells, and smiled.

"What will it be, mister?"

"Monongahela." Fargo had finished the bottle Brandy gave him and it whetted a hankering for more. "Don't bother with a glass." He leaned his elbows on the bar and felt warm fingers touch his.

"Well, look who it is."

Fargo almost didn't recognize Melissa Hart. She had done her hair up in bouffant fashion and wore a skintight dress covered in spangles. Her lips were cherry red and her eyelids were blue. "Well," he said.

"A girl has to earn a living, doesn't she?" Melissa stood so her bosom brushed his arm.

"I took you for a store clerk's or farmer's wife."

"Why? Because of my grandma? My grandpa was a farmer and look at where it got her. He died and she was left with pennies to her name and the farm had yet to be paid off." Melissa leaned back as he was doing. "It's why I brought her here. To help support her."

"What about your mother?"

"Consumption."

Fargo offered the bottle. "Care for a drink?"

"Don't mind if I do. But I like mine out of a glass." Melissa motioned at the barman, then leaned against him. "So. How does it feel to be the talk of Oro City?"

"I hope you're joking," Fargo said.

"You drove off those outlaws, didn't you? Everyone is talking about it. Or haven't you noticed the looks you've been getting?"

Fargo scowled at several men who chose that moment to point at him. He downed more coffin varnish.

"Have any plans for later tonight? If not, I give the best back rub this side of the Divide."

Fargo grinned. "You come right out with it." He liked that in a woman.

"Don't act surprised. As handsome as you are, you must be propositioned all the time." Melissa sipped and regarded a prospector in filthy clothes. "Plus you don't stink to high heaven. Half the time I have to hold my breath to keep from gagging."

"How long have you been in Oro City?"

"Pretty near a year. I worked at a saloon down the street until the Filmore opened. Luckily, the owner liked me. He pays better and he doesn't paw the help."

"You must know a lot of folks."

"I suppose I do." Melissa grinned and winked. "Most of them are men."

"Cobb and Whitten?"

"Oh." She stepped back. "Yes, I know both. Cobb better than Whitten."

"What are they like?"

"You can find out for yourself in about ten seconds how Gil Whitten is," Melissa said, and nodded. "Here he comes with his guard dog."

Two men were approaching. The first was as wide as a wall and as tall as a tree, with great sloping shoulders and huge hands. He wore a brown hat and had a six-shooter on his left hip. Behind him came a younger man in a suit and bowler. From under it poked curly dark hair. His mustache was neatly trimmed. In his left hand he twirled a cane with an ivory grip.

"I don't care to talk to him," Melissa said almost fearfully. "You're on your own." Turning, she melted in among the throng.

Fargo wondered what that was about. He shifted his arm so his right hand was near his Colt and held the bottle in his other hand.

The human hill stopped and moved aside for the dandy. "Mr. Whitten would like a word with you," he announced in a deep gravelly tone.

"Would he, now?"

"Yes, indeed," Gil Whitten said, holding out his hand and introducing himself. "Perhaps you've heard of me. I'm part owner of Cobb and Whitten Express."

Fargo shook.

"I was wondering if I might have a word with you." Whitten leaned on his cane.

"I aimed to have one with you tomorrow but here will do," Fargo said.

"Really? What about?"

"You first."

Whitten smiled. "Very well. Word is all over town about an incident you were involved in. Single-handedly you drove off five outlaws and brought in a stage belonging to our competitor."

"I'm right famous," Fargo said.

"I went to Dr. Jolsen's to talk to you but you had already left. He gave me a description and I asked around and someone recalled seeing you come in here."

"And now you've found me."

"Yes," Whitten said, taking no note of Fargo's sarcasm. "How about if I buy you a drink?"

Fargo waggled his bottle. "I already have one."

"Very well. I'll get straight to the point." Whitten cleared his throat. "I'd like to hire you as a driver."

"Not interested."

"Don't decide so quickly," Whitten said. "We pay fair wages and you'd have every other Sunday off."

"I already have a job offer."

"Might I ask from whom?"

"I suspect you already know."

"How could I?" Whitten rebutted. "We've only just met. But whoever it is, I'll double whatever they're paying you."

"It would make it easier for you, wouldn't it?" Fargo said. "She'd only have Rafer and the other one."

"I have no idea what you are talking about," Gil Whitten said.

"Brandy Randall," Fargo said. "I've agreed to lend her a hand."

"I'll triple the amount she's paying you."

"You want her out of business that much?"

"I never wish ill of anyone," Whitten said. "Think it over and get back to me in a day or two."

"I can get back to you now," Fargo said, and put a hand on his hurt leg. "I'm told that the bastards who did this work for you."

"Preposterous," Whitten said.

"I'm told that you're trying to drive Brandy out of business."

"Ridiculous," Whitten said.

"They say you're a mean son of a bitch who'd do anything to get what he wants."

"Where did you hear all this?"

"If it's true, if I find out you were to blame for me being shot, I'll pay you a visit."

"Was that a threat?"

"It sure as hell was."

"I see." Gil Whitten gnawed on his lip and tapped his cane on the floor and gazed about at the Filmore's patrons. "In that case I'll make it a point to continue this discussion at another time."

"You do that," Fargo said.

Whitten was red in the face. "Come along, Buchanan." Beckoning to his bodyguard, he threaded through the tables and out into the night.

The instant the batwings swung shut, Melissa Hart appeared.

"What was that all about? I couldn't hear what he said."

Fargo chugged some whiskey before he said, "You could have if you stayed."

"Him and me don't get along." Melissa smiled sweetly. "How about we talk about something else?"

Fargo let it drop, for now. He reckoned she would tell him in her own good time. "When are you done here?"

"Midnight."

"I'll stick around until then and walk you home."

Melissa put her hand on his chest. "I'd like that," she said. "I'd like that very much."

The minutes crawled. It didn't help that Fargo's wound wouldn't stop throbbing. It hurt worse than it had before the doc worked on him. He finished the second bottle and was tempted to buy a third but didn't. He sat in on a poker game but the cards were against him. He tried to buck the tiger and the tiger bucked him.

"I can take a hint," Fargo said to himself, and limped out for some fresh air. Leaning against a post, he cradled the Henry and was debating how to kill the half hour until Melissa was off when who should come strolling out but the lady herself.

"I got off early," she said, hooking her arm with his, "and I don't have to be back to work until one tomorrow. Do with me what you will."

"That covers a lot of territory," Fargo said.

"I know," Melissa said huskily, and laughed.

Her apartment was on the second floor of a building next to a bank. They had to climb a flight of outside stairs to reach her door. The windows were lit. Fargo figured she had left a lamp burning until he followed her in and there sat Edna, knitting in a rocking chair.

"You're still up, Grandma?" Melissa said, sounding disappointed.

"I couldn't sleep, child, after that awful business today." Edna placed her needles and part of a shawl in her lap and squinted. "Who's that with you, dear? My eyes aren't what they used to be."

"You remember Mr. Fargo? The gentleman who saved us from the stage robbers?"

"Oh, it is, isn't it?" Edna rose and came over and clasped Fargo's hand. "It's a pleasure to see you again, young man. Would you care for some tea or coffee?"

"No, thanks." Fargo looked at Melissa.

"Shouldn't you be getting to bed, Grandma? How about if I fix you a cup of warm milk? That always helps."

"It wouldn't tonight," Edna declared. "I'm too overwrought."

Fargo saw where this was going. "I guess I'll be on my way."

"Don't go," Melissa said. "Grandma will turn in sooner or later."

"Probably not for hours yet," Edna said.

Fargo limped out to the landing and Melissa came after him and clasped his wrist.

"I'm truly sorry. Usually she's in bed by now. Another time, then?"

"Another time," Fargo said in mild disgust. It had been a hell of a day and he might as well turn in. He descended the stairs and turned to go up the street.

Out of a doorway stepped a hulking form.

It was Buchanan.

6

Fargo was cradling the Henry instead of leaning on it. All he had to do was point and fire, and they both knew it.

Buchanan didn't try to draw his revolver. He didn't do anything but stand there and stare.

"What the hell do you want?" Fargo demanded.

"I didn't like how you talked to Mr. Whitten."

"He send you to warn me off?"

"He doesn't know I'm here. I came back on my own after I took him home."

"Why?"

Buchanan took a half step closer. "To give you a warnin' of my own. Mr. Whitten is a good man. I like workin' for him. You ever threaten him again, you'll answer to me."

"If he's so good, why is he out to destroy the Colorado Stage Company?"

"He's not."

"That's not what everyone else says."

"And I tell you that I'm with him every day and he's never said or done anything that would make me think that. Whoever told you is lyin'."

"Or you are," Fargo said.

Buchanan didn't get mad. He did a strange thing; he sighed. Then he said, "I've heard of you. You work mostly as a scout. You were in a shootin' match in Missouri a while back against some of the top shooters in the country."

Fargo let out a sigh of his own. It seemed like damn near everyone had heard about that match.

"From what I can gather, you're not an assassin. You don't hire out your gun for money. If I thought you did, if I thought you were brought here to kill Mr. Whitten, you wouldn't be standin' there. There have already been tries on his life."

"What?"

"I won't let there be another. He hired me to keep him alive and I always earn my pay."

"Who tried to kill him?"

"I have my suspicions," Buchanan said. "I used to be a lawman and I'm good at findin' things out. Consider this a friendly warnin'. You won't get another." He turned to go.

"Hold on," Fargo said. A vague recollection nipped at him. "Did you say lawman?"

"I wore a tin star down in Texas for about ten years," Buchanan revealed. "I quit about five years ago."

Fargo pried at his memory. "What's your full name?"

"James Buchanan."

"Big Jim Buchanan?" Fargo said, and suddenly it all came back to him. "Are you the one the newspapers used to write about? The Town Tamer?"

"Damn newspapers," Buchanan said.

Fargo studied him with new interest. Big Jim Buchanan was a Texas legend. A straight-arrow lawman who couldn't be bribed or scared off. Buchanan had cleaned up half a dozen of the toughest towns anywhere. Quick with his fists and his gun, he'd wiped out the notorious Amos Salk gang and with a handful of deputies had fought off thirty or forty Comanches in the Battle of Adobe Flats, as it was called. "I've heard of you, too."

"Then I don't have to tell you I mean what I say. Stay away from Gil Whitten." Buchanan strode off.

Fargo set the Henry's stock on the ground and leaned on it to spare his leg. He didn't know what to make of all this. On the one hand he had Brandy Randall, who claimed Whitten and Cobb were out to destroy her. On the other, he had a man with Buchanan's reputation claiming Whitten wasn't.

Fargo put it aside for the time being. He'd get to the bottom of the affair eventually, and when he did, there would be hell to pay.

The stage office was dark and quiet and the wide door to the stable stood partway open. Just inside was the stage. The Ovaro had been placed in a stall, Fargo's saddle and saddle blanket and saddlebags in a neat pile nearby. He spread out his bedroll, wearily sank onto his back, and no sooner closed his eyes than he was asleep.

For years Fargo's habit was to wake at the crack of dawn.

He sat up and stretched and grimaced at the dull ache in his leg. He checked the bandage as Doc Jolsen had advised; there was no fresh blood. Stiffly rising, he shuffled outside and over to a water trough. He removed his hat, took a breath, and plunged his head in. The water was chill and bracing. He rose up, dripping wet, and shook himself.

"You want a towel, mister? We have one in the office."

Fargo wiped his face with his sleeve and jammed his hat on.

The boy who had gone for the sawbones was eyeing him as if he might bite. "Jimmy, isn't it?"

"Yes, sir. Jimmy Hayes. I run errands for Miss Randall and help get the stage ready."

"She a good boss?"

"The best," Jimmy said. "She's the nicest lady ever. I'd do anything for her."

It sounded to Fargo as if the boy was smitten. "What do you do for breakfast around here?"

Jimmy pointed up the nearly empty street. "There's Betty's Kitchen yonder. She usually opens about this time and serves the best pancakes in creation."

Fargo left the Henry in the stable. He'd mend faster if he didn't baby himself. After only a block, though, his leg hurt as bad as the day before. He was glad to sit in a chair at a long table and downright tickled at the quality of Betty's coffee. He ordered half a dozen eggs with bacon and toast smeared with strawberry jam and had just forked his first mouthful when the door opened and in came his new boss.

"Morning. Jimmy told me I'd find you here." Brandy sat across from him. "Are you up to taking a stage out today?"

"Tomorrow would be better."

"Your leg? I understand. I'll take it myself, then. I've made the run plenty of times."

Fargo picked up a slice of bacon and bit off a juicy wedge of fat. "You didn't tell me that Big Jim Buchanan works for Gil Whitten."

Brandy sat back. "I don't know everybody they've hired. They must have fifty men on their payroll. Is he a driver?"

"A friend of mine called him Whitten's guard dog. That fits as good as anything."

"Why does Whitten need a guard?"

"Someone has been trying to kill him."

Brandy cocked her head. "Are you joshing me? How come I've never heard of any tries on his life?"

"Maybe Whitten kept them to himself."

"Hogwash," Brandy said. "Word would be all over Oro City. Ask around. I bet no one else has heard of it either."

Fargo dipped a slice of toast into an egg yolk. "I'll need an advance on my pay."

"How much?"

"A hundred dollars should do it." Fargo bit and chewed. Next to roast buffalo, eggs were about his favorite food.

"That's a lot," Brandy said.

"You offered to pay me twice the going rate," Fargo reminded her. "Top drivers earn that much a month."

"True," Brandy conceded. "But I run a small line, remember? My going rate is sixty. I've made an exception in your case because I'm desperate. How about if I give you sixty now and the rest after you've worked a week or so?"

"I need the hundred now."

Brandy's jaw muscles twitched and she drummed her fingers on the table. "Why on earth do you need that much?"

"For this and that," Fargo said.

"You're taking advantage of my good nature. You know that, don't you?"

"Don't pay me if you don't want to."

"And what? Have no one but me to drive my stages? You have me over a barrel, damn you." Brandy angrily pulled out a thin roll of bills. She peeled off most of them and slid the money across. "Here. I hope you're happy."

"I am."

When he didn't say more, Brandy stood. "I have to help get the stage ready. Do I have your word you'll take a run after I get back?"

"You do."

"Good."

Fargo watched her leave. She was upset about the advance but it couldn't be helped. He finished eating, paid, and limped out into the bright sunlight of the new morning. Shopkeepers were opening their stores. A farmer was unloading produce at a general store. He came to the first saloon but it was closed so he went on to the next. It was empty save for the barman who was sweeping the floor.

"We start serving at ten," the man said.

Fargo held out five of the hundred dollars. It wasn't much but he had a lot of saloons to visit. "This is yours if you'll do something for me."

"Last of the big spenders," the barman said, and went on sweeping. "What do I do to earn it?"

"I'm looking for a gent who wears a black duster and a man who is part Ute."

The man stopped sweeping. "That would make him a breed and breeds ain't allowed in here. The owner doesn't care for their kind." He plucked the five dollars from Fargo's fingers. "And do you have any notion of how many men wear dusters?"

"This one is a gun hand," Fargo said, "and he robs stagecoaches."

"Oh." The man glanced at Fargo's leg. "You're him. The gent who shot it out with those bandits."

"Get word to me at the Colorado Stage Company." Fargo was to the door when the man called to him.

"Are you fixing to spread your wealth all over town?"

"I am," Fargo admitted.

"Word will get around. Could be that the breed and that fella in the duster will hear of it and come looking for you."

"I hope they do," Fargo said.

It took the rest of the morning but Fargo used up ninety of the hundred and had eyes and ears at every saloon, two barbershops, and every store. His wound was itching abominably when he returned to the stable. Sitting on his saddle, he rolled up his pant leg, untied the bandage, and bent down. The sawbones had told him to watch if the skin changed color or for the veins around the holes to darken but there was no sign of infection. Relieved, he rewrapped the bandage good and tight.

A shadow played down the aisle and in came Rafer Barnes. "There you are! I've been lookin' all over for you."

"Any particular reason?"

"You'll never guess who showed up at the office a couple of hours ago wantin' to see you," Rafer said. "Gil Whitten and that bear of his, Buchanan. Thank God Brandy had left with the Denver stage or she'd have torn into him."

"Whitten say why he wanted to see me?"

"I asked but he told me it was none of my business."

Rafer might have gone on but just then a boy of ten or so appeared in the doorway. The boy was breathing hard and sweating and stood uncertainly glancing from one of them to the other.

"You want something?" Rafer said.

"Yes, sir."

"Well, out with it boy."

"Is one of you Mr. Fargo?"

"That would be me," Fargo said.

"My pa sent me. He runs the general store on Fourth Street. He sent me to tell you that a man in a black duster is there right this minute."

7

Fargo hadn't expected to hit pay dirt so soon. He followed the boy out, limping as fast as he could, and acquired a shadow at his elbow.

"Wasn't one of the owlhoots we tangled with a tall gent in a black duster?"

"I recollect there was."

"You crafty devil," Rafer complimented him. "But what are you goin' to do when we get there?"

"Cross that bridge," Fargo said.

"If it's him he's liable to shoot at us on sight," Rafer predicted.

"Hang back and let me take care of it."

"Not on your life. There's liable to be gunplay and I wouldn't miss it for the world."

"Ever hear how many bystanders are hit when lead starts to fly?"

"I'll duck."

The boy impatiently beckoned. "My pa said to hurry. He said he didn't know how long the man in the black duster would be there."

The store was named after the owner and called Benett's Emporium. Fargo remembered that it had narrow aisles and high shelves crammed with merchandise. He elected to stop under the overhang to a butcher shop next door. "Go in and see if the man is still there," he said to the boy. "But don't let on."

"What about the back door?" Rafer asked.

"Why would he go out the back? He doesn't know we're after him."

"I hope you're right."

Hardly a minute passed and the boy bounded out. "I asked my pa," he reported in a low voice, "and he says to tell you the man is still in there. He wanted ammunition and my pa stalled him by saying he had to get it out of the storeroom."

"I owe your pa another five," Fargo said. "Now you hunt cover."

The boy wheeled and ran back in.

"Damn it," Fargo said.

"You told him to hunt cover," Rafer chuckled. "You didn't say where."

Fargo sidled to the big front window. A woman was trying on bonnets and a man in overalls was examining a hammer. Neither noticed him.

"Anything?" Rafer whispered.

"You should make yourself scarce."

"I won't get anyone to buy me drinks at the saloons if I don't have stories to tell."

Fargo tore his gaze from the window. "It was you, wasn't it?"

"Me what?"

"Don't play innocent, damn you. You're the one who went all over town telling everyone about me running off the stage robbers."

"I might have mentioned it to a few folks here and there," Rafer said.

"Now everyone in Oro City knows."

"What's wrong with that? You should thank me for making you famous."

"I should kick you in the ass."

Fargo moved back to wait. It wasn't ten seconds later that a man in a black duster and flat-crowned black hat came out of the general store. In his left hand was a box of ammunition. He turned away from them and started up the street.

"That's him!" Rafer whispered.

Fargo stepped from under the overhang. The sun was so bright he had to squint. He put his hand on his Colt and called out, "Stop right there, mister."

The man looked over his shoulder and halted. His face was inscrutable in the shadow of his hat brim. "Are you talkin' to me?"

"Held up any stages lately?"

"You're loco." The man in black walked on.

"You put a slug in me, you son of a bitch."

The man stopped again, and turned. His face was no longer in shadow. He had a hard, almost cruel expression, and eyes the color of flint. "What did you just call me?"

"Ears not working?" Fargo said.

Somewhere behind him Rafer snickered.

The man slowly slid the ammunition into a pocket and just as slowly moved the right side of his duster to reveal an ivory-handled Smith & Wesson. "Mister, you have any idea what you just stepped in?"

"I'm real scared," Fargo said.

The man glanced at the position of the sun and shifted to the right. His thin lips curled in a mocking smile as if he knew something Fargo didn't. "You say I shot you. I say I didn't. How do you aim to prove which of us is tellin' the truth?"

"Easy," Fargo said. "Whoever is still breathing a minute from now."

"Fine by me."

Fargo was so intent on the man in black that he didn't notice someone had come up the street until a figure in a vest stepped between them.

"What the hell is going on here?" Marshal Shicklin demanded. He was holding a double-barreled shotgun. "Either of you unlimber your hardware and I will by God blow you in half."

"Don't look at me, Marshal," the man in the black duster said. "I was mindin' my own business and this hombre threatened to shoot me."

"Fargo?" Marshal Shicklin said.

"He's one of the stage robbers."

"You have proof?"

"Nothing that would stand up in court but if you arrest him we can—"

The marshal held up a hand. "Hold it right there. I enforce the law here, not you. And the law says I have to have proof before I can throw someone behind bars."

The man in the black duster grinned.

"Damn it," Fargo said. "You interfere in this and the next stage he robs will be on your head."

Shicklin faced the man in black. "You look familiar. Who the hell are you?"

"Jack Santor."

"Can you account for your whereabouts last evening when the stage was robbed?"

"I was with my employer."

"And who might he be?"

"You have a poor memory, Marshal," Santor said. "You saw me with him just last week." He paused. "I work for Bill Mercer."

"Oh hell," Marshal Shicklin said.

"Something the matter?" Fargo asked.

"William Mercer happens to be one of the richest men in Oro City. He owns the bank, for one thing, and has money invested in half of all the businesses, besides. He's law-abiding and churchgoing and the last person in the world who'd ever rob a stage."

"I didn't say he did."

"Enough. I'd arrest you for disturbing the peace but then I'd have to feed you and they make me pay for meals out of my own pocket."

"You could starve him," Jack Santor said.

Marshal Shicklin grunted. "Both of you will go your own ways. And Fargo, if you give me any more trouble, I'll take his suggestion and leave you in my jail until you rot."

"Some lawman," Rafer said.

"That goes for you too, old man."

"What did I do?"

"Skedaddle," Marshal Shicklin said. "Now."

Santor was already walking off. Fargo frowned and limped in the opposite direction, aware that the lawman was watching to be sure he went.

"The nerve of that tin star," Rafer said.

"You told me once that you don't trust him," Fargo mentioned, "but you never said why."

"There's rumors that he can be bought," Rafer said. "That if you pay him, he'll look the other way."

"This is some town you have here," Fargo said. But the truth be known, Oro City wasn't any different from most other frontier towns. Greed created them; the lust for gold or silver or anything else that reaps riches. Greed sustained them; the lust for the money of those looking for the gold or silver. When you got right down to it, he reflected, greed was the grease that lubricated civilization.

"There's more goin' on than I thought," Rafer said. "Take the feller that Santor works for—"

"William Mercer?"

"He's top dog. The marshal didn't stretch the truth a lick when he said that Mercer has his hands into just about all there is in Oro City."

"I should pay him a visit."

Rafer gripped Fargo's arm and stopped. "You don't want to do that, son."

"Why not?"

"Santor ain't the only cat-eyed hombre Mercer has workin' for him."

"What does a banker need with a pack of curly wolves?"

"From what I hear, he's been in a few scrapes with business rivals, I guess you'd call them."

They were almost to the Filmore House. "How about a drink?" Fargo suggested.

"This early in the day?"

"It's on me."

"I am plumb thirsty," Rafer said, and laughed.

Barely a score of gamblers and drinkers were at the tables and the bar. Fargo paid for a glass for each of them and they repaired to a table.

"Ahhhh," Rafer said after taking a sip. "This will get the blood flowin'."

"It's better than lead."

"What? Oh. Sure is. I can't drink as much as I used to on account of Brandy fires anyone who shows up for work drunk."

"Thanks for the warning."

"She won't fire you, hoss," Rafer said. "She needs your gun too much."

Melissa pulled out a chair. Today she had on a pink dress with white frills. It was cut so low in front, it was a wonder her breasts didn't pop out. "I'm sorry about last night."

"What happened last night?" Rafer asked.

41

"I wasn't talking to you, you old goat," Melissa said without looking at him. "Why don't you go spin the roulette wheel?"

"I never play roulette, girl. The odds are too high."

"Then go watch someone else play it."

"Why should I—?" Rafer stopped. "Oh. You want to talk to him alone." He pushed his chair back and stood. "Never let it be said Rafer Barnes ain't a gentleman."

"Get lost, damn it."

"You had no call to do that," Fargo said as Rafer drifted away.

"Yes, I did. What I have to say is for your ears and yours only." Melissa bent and lowered her voice. "There's a rumor going around."

"Another one?"

"I'm serious. I don't know how it started or who is to blame but it concerns you."

"Keep me in suspense, why don't you?"

Melissa nervously glanced about. "The new rumor is that someone has put a price on your head."

8

Fargo never put a lot of stock in gossip. People loved to bullshit; it was human nature. "Where did you hear it?"

Melissa shrugged. "I don't remember."

"Give me a name."

"You've seen how packed it gets in here. I talk to a lot of people. I don't always remember who says what."

Fargo was good at reading people. And his instincts told him she was lying. "I thought we were friends."

"We are," Melissa said, sounding hurt. "Why would you say a thing like that?"

"I want the truth."

"I gave it to you. I honestly don't remember who told me."

"What did you have for breakfast?" Fargo asked.

"Pancakes with maple—" Melissa stopped. Her cheeks turned pink and she pushed to her feet. "I try to warn you and you do this? You can just go to hell." Wheeling, she angrily strode off.

Rafer came from behind a couple of townsmen and took his seat. "Lover's spat?" he said, and chuckled.

"She claims someone has put a bounty on me."

Rafer's grin evaporated. "The hell you say. Where did she hear that?"

"She wouldn't tell me."

"That's damn peculiar."

Fargo nodded. "You must know a lot of folks hereabouts, as long as you've been here."

"I know a heap of people," Rafer boasted, and straightened. "Oh. I savvy. You want me to ask around, find out more about this rumor of hers?"

"I'd be obliged."

"Say no more." Rafer polished off his drink in a single gulp and got back up. "I don't need to tell you to watch your back."

"Always do," Fargo said. He took his time with his whiskey, sipping and pondering. In a way the rumor was encouraging. Whoever was behind putting lead into him was worried. He liked that. He wanted the son of a bitch to know that he was coming for him, and to sweat buckets. It wasn't enough that he find the gun hand who squeezed the trigger. He was after whoever hired the gun hand.

Tilting his glass, Fargo drained it and set it down. He rose and went out. The pain in his leg was a little less but he had to be careful not to put too much weight on it. By the time he reached the Colorado Stage Company he regretted not taking the Henry along.

Jimmy was in a chair under the overhang at the office, carving on a piece of wood. He smiled and held up a fair likeness of a horse. "What do you think?"

"You've got talent," Fargo said.

"I've got a whole collection," the boy said. "I'll show them to you sometime if you want."

"Sure."

"Maybe my ma will have you over for supper. She's a good cook."

Fargo didn't say anything.

"You wouldn't happen to be looking for a wife, would you?" Jimmy asked.

"Not today, no."

"That's too bad. I lost my pa a while back and Ma says I need a new one. She's been looking but she says she can't find anyone worth a hoot. She says a lot of men are only interested in one thing but she won't tell me what the one thing is."

Fargo elected to change the subject. "Anyone been around here this morning?"

"No, sir. I've been sitting here about an hour now and no one has come by."

Fargo walked on to the stable. He smelled the straw and the horses and saw the Ovaro looking at him and he was about to greet it when he realized the stallion was looking at the corner of the stable behind him and not at him. The Ovaro stamped a hoof.

Fargo whirled. He was almost around when a body slammed into him. A knife glittered, and he got hold of a wrist as he was slammed to the ground. A knee gouged his stomach.

Dark eyes fixed on him with fierce intensity, the same eyes that had glared at him through Brandy's window. His attacker had on store-bought clothes any white man would wear and his hair was cut white-fashion but his features and his skin left no doubt; it was the half-breed.

The breed hissed and the tip of the blade dipped within a whisker of Fargo's throat. With a powerful heave Fargo threw the man off and rolled, drawing his Colt as he rose. The knife flashed at his wrist. He jerked his arm aside and the blade struck the Colt so hard, the revolver was knocked from his grasp.

Uttering another feral hiss, the breed was on him. Fargo scrambled back, his wounded leg flaring with pain. The blade streaked at his face. He twisted, scrambled out of reach, slid his right hand under his right pant leg. His back was to a stall.

The half-breed crouched. Grinning, he moved the knife in small circles. Then he did something no warrior in a life-or-death fight would do. He spoke. "Going to kill you, white man."

"Think so?" Fargo said, and showed what he held in his right hand. He'd drawn the Arkansas toothpick that he kept in an ankle sheath.

It gave the breed pause. Then he glanced at Fargo's wounded leg, and grinned anew. "You hurt. Not move quick." He feinted with his knife. "Me very quick."

Fargo replied with, "If you were any slower you'd be a turtle."

The breed sprang. Fargo countered. Their blades rang and the breed skipped back. Fargo wagged the toothpick as the breed had wagged the knife. The breed came in low and slashed. Again steel pealed on steel. Again the breed bounded away.

"Not as easy as you'd thought it would be, is it?" Fargo taunted.

The breed liked to hiss. He thrust left and shammed shifting to the right but continued left. Fargo sidestepped but he wasn't quite fast enough and felt a slight sting in his side. The blade had cut his shirt and skin but not gone deep.

The breed darted back and smirked. "Me plenty quick, eh?"

Fargo was glad for the stall at his back. The breed couldn't try to get behind him. Hampered as he was by his leg, he might not be able to turn in time.

The breed shifted right. He shifted left. He was seeking an opening. He stopped and scowled and glanced at the entrance as if wary of being discovered.

"Afraid?" Fargo baited him.

Without any warning the man hurtled at him. Fargo deflected a cut at his throat and was nicked in the arm. A foot rammed his wounded leg and he nearly cried out. His leg buckled and he would have fallen but the breed had hold of his wrist. He grabbed the breed's. Exerting every sinew, Fargo threw the man from him.

The breed stumbled a few feet and recovered. He was angry at being thwarted and did something else no warrior would do—he swore.

"Mr. Fargo?"

Fargo froze in consternation. Jimmy was in the door, the wooden horse in one hand, his knife in the other. "Get out of here!" he shouted.

The boy never stood a prayer. The breed spun and was on him in swift bounds. Jimmy grunted as the breed's blade sank to the hilt in his chest. Without breaking stride, the breed yanked it out and was past the door.

"No!" Fargo ran as best he could. He reached Jimmy as the boy, his face contorted in shock, fell to his knees with a hand to his chest and blood spurting.

Fargo caught him. "I have you," he said, helplessness washing over him.

"Why—?" Jimmy gurgled, and scarlet flecked his lips and dribbled down his chin. His eyes widened and he exhaled and was gone.

Fargo held him a full minute before lowering the body to the ground. A boundless rage had set his temples to pounding. Rage at the half-breed and at the man who sent him. He almost didn't hear the click of a gun hammer.

"Put the knife down and raise your hands where I can see them."

Fargo looked into the muzzle of Marshal Shicklin's Remington. "I didn't do this."

"I won't tell you twice," the lawman warned.

Fargo let the toothpick drop and elevated his arms. "Didn't you see the half-breed run off?"

"I just got here. I didn't see anyone but you and the boy." Shicklin sidled around to where he could see Jimmy better. His face became stone. "I know his ma. This will break her heart. She's already lost her husband." He glared at Fargo. "Give me an excuse, big man. Give me any excuse at all."

"I tell you I didn't do it."

"I saw you bent over the boy with my own eyes, still holding the knife you killed him with."

"It was the breed, damn it."

"What breed?" Shicklin glanced about. "Sounds to me like you're making it up to save your ass." He motioned. "On your feet."

Fargo complied, saying, "Take a look at my side and my arm. You can see I've been cut. The breed attacked me in the stable and then stabbed Jimmy."

"Is that what you're going to tell the judge?" Marshal Shicklin said contemptuously. "It doesn't wash with me and it won't wash with him." He motioned again. "Turn around. I'm taking you to jail."

Seething with frustration, Fargo moved toward the office. "You're making a mistake."

"I've made them before and I never lose any sleep over them. But I've got to be careful. There are some on the council who think I make too many. Which is why I'm not letting you go."

"Damn you. Is that all you care about, your badge?"

"I'd watch my mouth, boy killer. But as a matter of fact, it is. I'd do anything to keep wearing this tin. It's all I have."

Fargo angled toward the office so he would pass within a step or two of the post at the near end of the overhang. He exaggerated his limp and slowed and asked, "What will it take to convince you?"

"Nothing you can do or say will . . ." The lawman abruptly fell silent.

"What?"

"I ran into Rafer."

"And?"

"He asked me if I'd heard a rumor going around that someone put a price on your head. I hadn't, and I came here to see you about it."

"That must be why the breed jumped me." Fargo looked over his shoulder. "*Now* will you believe that I didn't kill the boy?"

"Whether you're innocent or guilty is for a court to decide," Shicklin stubbornly maintained. "I have to go by the evidence of my own eyes."

"That's too bad," Fargo said.

By then they were at the post.

9

Fargo had to time it just right. He sprang, using his good leg, wrapped both hands around the post, and whipped his legs up and around.

Marshal Shicklin had gazed off up the street and was a shade slow in reacting. He started to point his six-shooter just as Fargo's boots slammed into his chest. Shicklin's own boots left the earth and he was smashed onto his back. The few seconds he lay stunned were enough for Fargo to reach him and snatch the Colt from under the lawman's belt.

Fargo jammed the muzzle against Shicklin's neck and thumbed back the hammer. "Don't so much as twitch."

The lawman's eyes focused and anger turned his face beet red. "You son of a bitch."

Fargo relieved him of the Remington and jammed it under his belt. Limping back, he commanded, "On your feet."

"This will only make it worse."

"Let me worry about that."

"Who knows? Maybe you're right and the jury will believe you didn't do it."

"Get the hell up." Fargo knew Shicklin was stalling in the hope that someone would notice and yell for help.

Grunting, the marshal rose and started to brush himself off.

"Enough of that," Fargo said, and shoved him toward the stable.

Shicklin reluctantly moved. "For an innocent man you act awful guilty."

"I have to find the breed who killed Jimmy and I can't do it behind bars."

"What do you aim to do with me?"

"I won't kill you unless you make me," Fargo said. "So be smart and behave."

They entered and Fargo told him to walk down the aisle to where his saddle and bedroll were piled and to sit with his back to the stall. Keeping him covered, Fargo got his rope.

Shicklin wasn't happy. "When folks find out about this, I'll be a laughingstock."

"At least you'll be breathing." Fargo began to uncoil the rope.

"You don't understand." Marshal Shicklin hesitated. "I'm not well liked."

"There's a shock."

"I told you I'm fond of my job. I want to keep it and if this gets around, there are a few who would use it as an excuse to get rid of me."

"Poor you," Fargo said, still unraveling.

"How about we strike a deal?"

Fargo snorted.

"I mean it. You let me go and I won't say anything about any of this."

"I wasn't born yesterday."

"Damn you. It's in my own interest, isn't it? All I ask is that you trust me."

"Like you trusted me."

"Once I'm gone, send someone to fetch me. Tell that story about the breed. I won't arrest you. You'll be free to go on doing whatever you're up to and I get to go on wearing my badge."

"You almost sound serious."

"I am."

Fargo looked at him. He'd met a lot of law dogs in his travels. Good ones, crooked ones, some who weren't worth a hoot and shouldn't be wearing tin. "You're a miserable bastard, Shicklin. Do you know that?"

"So I'll do anything to protect my ass. So what? That doesn't make me worthless. I enforce the law the best I can. And I'm always fair."

The hell of it was, Fargo realized, the man believed his own words. "No deal. I'll tie you and throw you in the tack room and then I'm going after the breed."

Shicklin considered a few moments. "How about I give you something in exchange for letting me go?"

"You don't have anything I want."

"I have information. I know things most people don't. I'll share some of it if you agree to letting me go."

Fargo was interested despite himself. "Let me hear it."

"This stagecoach war."

"What about it?"

Shicklin glanced at the door. "There have been a couple of attempts on Gil Whitten's life."

"I already know that."

"Oh. Then how about this? Do you also know that there is a third partner in the Cobb and Whitten stage line? A silent partner. A man who put up most of the money to start the company and has more of a stake in it than they do."

"His name?"

"William Mercer."

Fargo mulled that.

"How about it?" Shicklin impatiently asked. "Do we have our deal or not? The boy's body won't lie out there unnoticed forever."

Fargo twirled his Colt into his holster. He took the Remington, unloaded it, spun it so the grips were to the lawman. "Get out of here."

Shicklin grabbed the revolver and hurried to the door. He stopped to look back. "One more thing. The name of the breed you're looking for is Tangwaci. Tangwaci Smith, if you can believe it." He hustled off.

Fargo took a step after him but stopped. "Son of a bitch." The lawman knew a lot more than he let on. They needed to have another talk, and soon.

For now, Fargo set down his rope and went out. He avoided looking at Jimmy and limped past the office and down the street to the first person he came to, a middle-aged townsman in a bowler. "Mister, I can use your help."

The man stared at him as if he might have a disease. "Help you how?"

"Can you fetch the marshal? I'd go myself but I can't run very fast with this leg of mine."

"I saw you favoring it. What do you need Marshal Shicklin for?"

"There's been a stabbing."

The man was suddenly a concerned citizen. "Who's been stabbed? And who stabbed him? Where did it happen? Did you see it?"

"The marshal," Fargo said. "Will you bring him?"

"Certainly."

Fargo returned to the stage office. There was a cot against a wall for the drivers to use. He helped himself to a blanket and used it to cover Jimmy's body. Since there was nothing else he could do, he sat in the chair the boy had been whittling in.

It wasn't long before boots pounded and Marshal Shicklin arrived with the townsman. Fargo pointed without saying anything and Shicklin went to the body and raised the blanket. The townsman gasped. Shicklin sent him to bring a deputy and others and then came over. He was grinning.

"I'm as good as my word."

"Try not to shed any tears over the boy."

"I don't shed tears over anybody."

"Another shock," Fargo said.

Word spread quickly. In no time a crowd had gathered.

Doc Jolsen examined the body and announced that the boy had indeed been stabbed to death. About then the mother arrived and her wail cut through Fargo like a knife. Friends tried to comfort her but she was inconsolable. The undertaker was given the task of removing her son.

Through it all, Fargo sat in the chair. A man who worked for the *Oro Gazette* asked his side of things and he told about being attacked by a breed and how the breed had stabbed poor Jimmy.

"Any idea why this breed wanted you dead?"

"None at all," Fargo lied.

"Maybe he was out to rob you," the newspaperman suggested, and scribbled on his pad.

Fargo was glad when everyone finally dispersed. The last to leave was Marshal Shicklin. He had his thumbs hooked in his gun belt and was pleased with himself.

"Went as slick as could be, don't you think?"

"Shouldn't you be hunting for Tangwaci Smith?"

Shicklin lowered his hands. "Why are you treating me like I'm dirt? I kept my word, didn't I?"

"You knew about Smith all along."

"We don't have many breeds in Oro City. There's an old woman who is part Crow who does laundry. There's a girl who is part white and part Cheyenne. And then there's Tangwaci. He's a bad apple. It wasn't hard to figure out which one it might be."

"Go away," Fargo said.

The lawman sniffed. "One day someone is going to take you down a peg," he predicted, and walked off.

Fargo stayed in the chair until Shicklin was out of sight. Then he rose and went to the stable. He paused to stare at the red stain. "He won't get away with it, boy," he vowed.

The sawbones had told him not to ride for a while but Fargo had things to do. He slid a bridle on and brought the Ovaro out. He threw on the saddle blanket and the saddle and tightened the cinch and was leading the stallion outside when Rafer Barnes came puffing up the street.

"What's this I hear about Jimmy?"

Fargo gave a brief account.

"God, no. I liked that boy. He was always respectful, always eager to please." He glanced at the Ovaro. "Say, where are you off to?"

"Where do I find William Mercer?"

"At his bank or his house. The bank is on Sixth Street. His house is at the west edge of town. You can't miss it. It looks like a pine mansion."

"Thanks." Fargo gripped the saddle horn with both hands and pulled himself up and over. Pain lanced his leg but only until he hooked his boot in the stirrup.

"Be careful," Rafer cautioned. "Jack Santor is liable to be with him, along with a bunch of others. Mercer gives them the word, they'll tear into you."

"They'll try." Fargo lifted the reins. "Keep watch here until I get back."

"Wait. Don't you want to hear what I found out?"

Fargo had almost forgotten. "That's right. You were going to ask around."

"I asked everywhere. Every saloon. Everyone I knew who I ran into."

"And?" Fargo prompted when Rafer didn't go on.

"You're sure that dove said there was a price on your head?"

"Her exact words."

"Strange," Rafer said. "Because no one I talked to heard of it. Not even the bartenders and they hear pretty much everything."

"Maybe it hasn't gotten around yet."

"Then how did she hear about it?" Rafer shook his head. "No, she was lyin' or bein' contrary."

"Why would she make up something like that?" Fargo wondered out loud.

"How would I know? She's female and females are peculiar critters."

A thought struck Fargo. "If there's no bounty, why did that breed try to kill me?"

"Breeds are peculiar, too."

"You're a big help." Fargo reined around.

"Bounty or no bounty," Rafer said, "you'd best have eyes in the back of your head from here on out."

"I hear that," Fargo said.

10

"Pine mansion" was a good description. Three stories high with gables and arches and even a balcony, it was the most impressive structure in Oro City. Fargo had never seen anything quite like it. He rode up a treelined private road to the foot of wide slate steps. Dismounting, he tied off the reins on the hitch rail and had his boot on the first step when the front door opened and a portly white-haired butler in a uniform emerged.

"May I help you, sir?"

"I'm here to see Mercer," Fargo said as he climbed.

"Mr. Mercer is usually at the bank this time of the day," the butler informed him.

"I stopped there and they told me he was here."

The butler covered well. Without changing expression he said, "Perhaps he came home and I wasn't aware. Permit me to check."

"You do that."

A long hall led into the interior. Fargo leaned against the wall and saw the butler enter a room four doors down on the left. He figured the man would come back and tell him Mercer wasn't home but his hunch proved wrong.

"Mr. Mercer is in his study, sir. He says for me to escort you."

On the hall wall was a painting of a voluptuous young woman in a flowing lacy robe that left little to the imagination.

"Mrs. Mercer must love this one," Fargo said.

"There is no Mrs. Mercer, sir," the butler replied. "Mr. Mercer has never married."

"As much money as he has, I'm surprised he doesn't have to beat women off with a stick."

The butler allowed the suggestion of a smile to curl his lips. "Mr. Mercer says that money is better than any woman could ever be."

Fargo was surprised the butler would admit it. "Do you agree?"

"I'm married, sir, and we have five children." He gave a slight bow and a sweep of his arm. "Here we are, sir. Have a nice day."

Across a spacious room was a mahogany desk. Behind it sat a man who was almost as wide and none of it was muscle. His moon face was as smooth as a baby's bottom. Round brown eyes gave him an owlish look.

"Come on in," the plump, overfed owl said.

Fargo took several steps and stopped. Two men were lounging in chairs to one side. Both wore revolvers. One of them was Jack Santor.

Santor grinned.

"What can I do for you?" William Mercer asked.

Fargo walked past the chairs. He didn't like having Santor and the other man at his back, and he shifted so he could keep an eye on them.

"Cat got your tongue?"

"Are these your nursemaids?"

Mercer looked at the gun hands. "What kind of question is that? Who are you and what do you want? I'm a very busy man who doesn't like having his time wasted."

"I came to ask you about Tangwaci Smith."

"Who?"

"He's part Ute, part white," Fargo said, "and he's on your payroll."

"I have no half-breed in my employ. Who claims I do?"

Fargo didn't answer.

"Whoever told you is mistaken. I would never hire a breed. I despise mixed bloods."

Fargo jerked a thumb. "You hire men like him."

"Mr. Santor? How is that pertinent? He's not a breed. Do you know him?"

"We've talked."

Santor sat up. "He's the one I told you about, Mr. Mercer.

Remember? He was all set to draw on me but the marshal stepped in."

"Not the gentleman who accused you of trying to rob the stage?"

"The same," Santor said, "and he ain't no gentleman by a long shot."

Mercer folded hands as plump as dumplings on his desk. "And now you show up in my home. What am I to make of all this, sir?"

"Playing me for a fool is a mistake," Fargo said.

"As is insulting me and accosting those who work for me," Mercer countered.

"You sent Tangwaci Smith to kill me."

"That's absurd," Mercer said. "I'm a banker. I don't kill people. And if I did, I wouldn't hire a half-breed to do the killing."

"You'd have Santor and his friends do it."

"I hired them to protect me, you cretin. Not to do harm to others."

"Next you'll tell me there have been attempts on your life," Fargo said sarcastically.

"As a matter of fact, there have. A month ago someone took a shot at me. Then about two weeks ago I stepped outside late one evening and a knife missed my head and stuck in the door."

Could it be? Fargo wondered. He sensed that the banker was telling the truth. Yet that meant that someone had tried to kill Mercer *and* Gil Whitten *and* Brandy.

"If there is nothing else, I'll thank you to leave." Mercer snapped his thick fingers at his hired guns. "If you would be so kind as to see him out."

"With pleasure," Santor said.

"One last question," Fargo said to Mercer. "Do you know any reason why anyone would want you dead?"

"Are you wealthy, Mr.—?"

"Fargo. I scout for a living. Scouts seldom get rich."

"Should you ever become so, you will find that people don't need a reason to try to take your money. Relatives, your business associates, complete strangers, all are out to bleed you dry. Wealth can be a curse as well as a blessing."

"So you're saying there are a lot of people who might want you dead?"

"If they could get their hands on my wealth by burying me, they would, yes." Mercer nodded at Santor. "Mr. Fargo is leaving now."

"You heard Mr. Mercer," Jack Santor said. He rose, his posture that of a snake coiled to strike, his hand poised close to his six-gun.

The other man was tensed to draw but he wasn't as obvious about it.

Fargo turned and walked out. Now wasn't the time or the place to confront Santor again. The butler was waiting in the hall and gave another of his little bows.

"This way, sir."

Fargo glanced back. Santor grinned and made a gesture.

"Another time," Fargo said.

"Whenever you have a hankering to die, come see me," Santor taunted.

Fargo was a few yards from the front door when he realized he was overlooking a chance to get at the truth. "Tell me something," he said to the butler. "How honest is Mercer?"

"Honest how, sir?"

"Would you trust him with your life? With your wife? With your last dollar?"

The butler grinned. "That would be something, Mr. Mercer needing money from me. As for the other, I shouldn't say this, but he's not the president who chopped down the cherry tree."

"Do you believe someone tried to kill him?"

"I more than believe it," the butler said. "I was there when he was shot at. I heard the rifle and then I heard the bullet strike. It's a wonder he wasn't killed."

"No one saw the shooter?"

"No, sir. Whoever it was, they were off in the trees. Mr. Mercer let the marshal know and Marshal Shicklin organized a posse and they searched the woods high and low but never found any sign."

Fargo didn't know what to make of it. The whole situation grew more complicated by the day. He put it from his mind on his ride into Oro City and drew rein at the Filmore House.

It was early but he could use a drink. He leaned on the bar and ordered a whiskey and savored his first sip. When a hand fell on his shoulder he didn't have to turn around to see who it was; he saw her reflection in the mirror. "Melissa."

"You're looking as handsome as ever." She pressed against him and traced the edge of his ear with her finger.

"I thought you were mad at me."

"I may have been but I never stay mad long." Melissa grinned and played with his hair. "You're not mad at me, are you?"

Fargo turned into her and put his arms around her waist. "Are you working?"

"Not for an hour yet. Why?"

"Where's your grandma?"

"At our place. She was knitting when I left."

"Hell," Fargo said.

"I truly am sorry about last night." Melissa brushed his neck with her lips. "I'd like to make it up to you. Do you have a room?"

Fargo recalled that Brandy wouldn't be back from Denver for another day yet. He took Melissa's hand. "Let's go for a walk."

Melissa giggled. "Just so I'm back in time. I can't afford to be fired."

Fargo untied the reins and led the Ovaro. The afternoon sun was hot. Dust swirled in the street. A horse drank loudly from a trough and a pig rooted at a hole under a porch.

"I just woke up half an hour ago," Melissa said. "What have you been up to today?"

"Not much of anything," Fargo said, and pulled her against him so their hips rubbed as they walked.

"Is it me or are you feeling frisky?"

Fargo would have cupped her bottom but for all the people.

"Frisky as hell."

"Frisky is good," Melissa said. "Frisky men are more fun and I hate being bored."

All the times Fargo had been with a woman, he couldn't recollect ever being bored. Even the ones who lay there like logs and didn't do much still got him excited enough to do what needed doing.

Out of the blue Melissa said, "I heard you paid a visit to William Mercer today."

"From who?"

"I don't remember."

Fargo looked at her. She smiled as innocently as a newborn. "What?"

"Nothing," Fargo said.

"I'm sorry I don't remember things but I don't have the best memory in the world."

Fargo roved his gaze from the twin bulges of her breasts down over her slim waist and the long sweep of her thighs. "You have other charms."

Melissa clasped his hand in both of hers and squeezed. "I shouldn't admit this but since last night all I can think about is you and me."

"We didn't do anything."

"I wanted to, though," Melissa said. "I wanted you as much as I've ever wanted any man."

"You don't say," Fargo said, pretending to be flattered. If she could playact so could he.

Melissa kissed him on the cheek and whispered in his ear, "I can't wait for you to get up under my dress."

"Makes two of us," Fargo said.

11

"Here?" Melissa said in disbelief after Fargo had put the Ovaro in the stable and brought her to the office.

"No one is around." Fargo closed and bolted the door and drew the burgundy curtains that Brandy must have hung to decorate the place.

"Here?" Melissa said again.

Slivers of light streamed past the edges of the curtains and dust motes sparkled in the air.

"Do you want to or not?" Fargo stood in front of her. "If you do, quit your complaining."

"It's just that what if someone comes?" Melissa asked, glancing nervously at the door.

"They'll knock and when we don't answer they'll figure no one is here and go away." Fargo put his arm around her and pulled her to him.

"But what if it's someone who works here?"

"The woman who owns the company took a stage to Denver. One driver is off drinking and the other is home nursing a busted foot."

"I'm sorry," Melissa said. "I just don't know if I can. I like a place that's more private."

Fargo kissed her anyway. She didn't respond at first but when he ran his hand over her bottom and then cupped a breast, she cooed softly in her throat and her breath and her body warmed. When he broke the kiss her eyes were closed.

"Mmmmm. I liked that."

"There's more," Fargo said, and kissed her again while roaming his hand up her thigh and caressing her through her dress.

Melissa grew hotter still. Her lips parted and her wet tongue met his. He sucked on it and she ground against him and panted into his mouth.

"God, you're a good kisser. Has anyone ever told you that?"

"You talk too much," Fargo said, and quieted her for a while with more kisses and more caressing. He grew rock hard.

Suddenly she placed her hand on his pole and he felt a lump in his throat.

"Oh my. I've struck pay dirt. Is this a sword in your pants?"

Fargo kissed and licked her neck and nipped at her left earlobe and then her right. She arched her back and played with the short hairs at the nape of his neck while stroking him down low.

"Nice," Melissa said. "Very nice." She giggled. "If this was made of wood there would be enough to burn the whole winter."

Fargo thought that a ridiculous thing to say but he kept it to himself. No sense in spoiling her mood. Scooping her into his arms, he lowered her to the cot. It creaked under their combined weight and dipped in the center.

"This isn't very comfortable," Melissa complained.

Fargo pressed his mouth to the junction of her cleavage. She tasted of perfume and powder.

Melissa shifted under him. "Something is poking me. I can't get comfortable."

"Hell," Fargo said. Picking her up again, he kicked the cot over and the blankets spilled onto the floor. A few flicks of his boot and he spread them enough to lay her back down. "Anything poking you now?"

"No, but a bed would be softer."

Fargo covered her mouth with his and began unbuttoning. It took a while. He hated dresses with a lot of buttons and hers had dozens. Finally he got the last button undone and peeled the dress from her shoulders. She wriggled to help him.

Underneath she wore a chemise. Another delay, and her breasts swelled free and he inhaled a nipple and flicked it with his tongue.

"Oh, yessssss," Melissa breathed, digging her fingernails into his shoulders.

Fargo gave each of her mounds attention while his hands

were busy below. He rubbed from her knee to her hip and then slid his hand between her velvet thighs and cupped her nether mount.

Melissa threw back her head and gasped.

Fargo parted her nether lips. He rubbed her tiny knob and her nails became daggers.

"Yes! There! There!"

A turn of Fargo's wrist and he plunged a finger into her wet sheath. For a few heartbeats she lay still, scarcely breathing. Then she gripped his hair hard enough to pull it out by the roots and thrust against him.

"I want you in me. Your sword."

Easing onto his knees, Fargo undid his gun belt and his pants. He rubbed himself along her, inserted the tip, and tensed.

"What are you waiting for?"

Fargo rammed up into her.

Melissa came up off the floor, her mouth an inviting oval, her eyes wide. "Oh baby! Give it to Momma!"

Their coupling was a heated medley of fingers and lips and the ever increasing urgency of their release. Rocking faster and faster, Fargo swept them to the brink. She crested first, gasping and groaning as she churned and bucked.

Fargo held off as long as he could. He liked to savor sex like he savored good whiskey. But there always came a point when there was no holding back even if he wanted to. He exploded and she cried out and drew blood with her nails.

Together they coasted to a stop. Fargo slid onto his side and rested his cheek on her shoulder and succumbed to the pull of sleep.

A sound brought him back. It was Melissa, snoring. He sat up and scratched his beard and was about to sink back down when a shadow passed across the window. Pulling his pants up, he buckled on his gun belt and quietly went to the window and parted the burgundy curtains. No one was out there. He was turning to go back to Melissa when he heard a sound. It seemed to come from the stable.

Fargo let her sleep. He saw no sense in disturbing her when it might be nothing. Jamming his hat on, he slid the bolt and cracked the door. The sun's glare made him squint. He poked his head out and heard the sound again. This time there was no doubt. Someone was in the stable.

Fargo slipped from the office. He crept to the corner. Inside the stable a shadow moved. Careful not to jingle his spurs, he stalked to the stable door. Two men were partway down the aisle. One was broad and wore a tailored dress coat and impeccable pants. His shoes were polished to a sheen. The other was a beanpole with gangly limbs. Neither was armed. Fargo stepped around the door. "Need something, gents?"

The beanpole gave him a cold stare but the heavyset one smiled and said, "If you work for the Colorado Stage Company, you certainly may. Who do we see about booking the next stage to Denver?"

"I can take down your names so you're first on the list," Fargo offered.

"How much is our fare?"

"I wouldn't know."

"You work for the stage line and you don't know how much they charge?" the skinny one asked.

"I just hired on," Fargo told them. "I'll get a paper and pencil and take your names." He remembered seeing both on Brandy's desk. In order not to wake Melissa he inched the door open. She stirred and mumbled. He found what he needed and went on back.

The pair were at the Ovaro's stall. The broad one was trying to pat its neck but the stallion had moved as far back as it could.

"Enough of that," Fargo said.

"A magnificent animal," the broad man said. "Is it yours?"

"Sure is," Fargo said with considerable pride. He stepped past them and the stallion came to him and he patted its neck.

"I do so admire superior horseflesh," the broad man said. "Almost as much as I like only the finest clothes and the best food. I'm Miles Blackburn, by the way, and my friend here is Mr. Hitch."

Fargo turned. He would take their names and get back to Melissa.

"We are purveyors of violence for a price."

"You do what?" Fargo wasn't sure he'd heard right.

64

"We hurt people," Miles Blackburn said. "You, for instance." And he speared his thick fingers out and up.

Fargo was caught flat-footed. The blow caught him in the ribs and torment exploded. Instinctively he backed away but he had nowhere to go; he backed into the stall. Letting the paper and the pencil drop, he stabbed for his Colt.

Hitch performed a remarkable feat. He jumped straight up into the air and lashed out with his right boot.

Pain burst in Fargo's chin. His legs buckled and he grabbed at the stall to stay on his feet. He stabbed for his Colt again but a thick hand was plucking it from his holster.

He lunged, and Hitch kicked him in the side. For someone so skinny, Hitch's kicks were immensely powerful. Fargo doubled over.

"We were hired to deliver a message, Mr. Fargo," Miles Blackburn said. He gripped Fargo's chin and raised his head.

"Yes, we know who you are. We are quite thorough, Mr. Hitch and myself." Blackburn squeezed, his fingers a vise. "Can you guess what the message is?"

Fargo kicked him in the knee. Blackburn let go and took a step back and Fargo went after him but Hitch stuck a leg out and the next thing Fargo knew, he was on his hands and knees and a boot was planted in his middle. He folded, or would have, except that Blackburn grabbed the back of his shirt and in a display of incredible brute strength, lifted him shoulder high and smashed him to the earth.

Fargo barely stayed conscious. The stable spun. He tried to rise but something heavy was on his back, pinning him. He tasted dirt.

"Don't pass out yet," Miles Blackburn said. "We're not done delivering our message."

Fargo was yanked erect and shaken until his teeth rattled. He balled his fists.

"Before I go, I must warn you," Blackburn was saying. "This is business. We are paid, we do our job, and we go. Should you make this personal, should you come after us, then we will make it personal, as well. Do you follow me?"

Fargo slugged him. It had no more effect than if he hit a wall. He cocked his arm to punch again but Hitch seized his wrist.

"Behave or I will break your arm," Miles Blackburn said.

"Who sent you?" Fargo managed to croak.

"We don't ever divulge that information." Blackburn pushed Fargo against a timber. "It won't do you any good to try to find out, either. Indeed, should you attempt to do so, there will be dire consequences."

Fargo girded his legs. He flashed a right cross at Blackburn but Hitch deflected his arm and kneed him. Pitching to his knees, Fargo clutched himself.

"You're a slow learner," Blackburn said.

"Go to hell," Fargo spat between clenched teeth.

"Honestly." Blackburn stepped back. "Our message is this. You are to stop sticking your nose into the stagecoach business. You are to leave Oro City and never return. And you have until midnight to do it."

"And if I don't?"

"Mr. Hitch and I will pay you another visit, only it won't be pleasant like this one." Blackburn smiled at his companion. "If you would be so kind to show him what we mean."

Hitch's leg was a blur.

Fargo's head seemed to cave in and the world blinked to black.

12

Something cool was on Fargo's forehead. A hand was stroking his hair. He opened his eyes and winced at a stab of pain.

"How bad are you hurt?" Melissa asked. She was cradling his head in her lap and pressing a wet rag to his forehead. "Should I fetch the doctor?"

Fargo tried to speak but his mouth was too dry. Moistening his lips, he said, "Where are they?"

"Where are who? I woke up a while ago and you were gone, so I got dressed and came out to look for you." Melissa bent over his head. "You have a bump the size of a goose egg."

Fargo groped at his holster. It was empty.

"Are you looking for this?" Melissa held up his Colt. "It was on the ground." She shoved it into the holster. "Someone sure beat on you good."

"Ever hear of two men called Blackburn and Hitch?"

"Oh, my God. It was them?" Melissa put a hand to her throat. "You don't want to tangle with those two."

Feeling—and more pain—spread through Fargo's body. He felt as if he had been stomped by a buffalo. "Tell me about them."

"I hear tell they're from New York City or some such. Word has it they hire out on the shady side of the law. You wouldn't know it to look at them but they are vicious. Most everyone is afraid of them."

"Where do I find them?"

"You don't, if you're smart." Melissa dipped the rag in a bucket, wrung it out, and placed it on his forehead.

"They have to live somewhere."

"I wouldn't know where that is. They're very secretive.

It wouldn't be healthy to snoop around trying to find them, either."

Fargo sat up. He gave the rag to Melissa and made it to his feet.

"Should you be up and about?"

Fargo strode out. He touched the goose egg and made a silent vow.

"Is there anything I can get you?"

"A bottle," Fargo said, and reconsidered. "On second thought, I'll get it myself. Come on. I'll walk you to the Filmore."

Melissa linked arms but looked at him as if he might bite her. She contained her curiosity for all of twenty steps. "What are you planning to do?"

"What do you think?" Fargo scanned the street but the pair were long gone.

"To tell the truth, you're scaring me. The tone of your voice, your eyes."

Fargo adjusted his hat.

"You aim to kill them, don't you? But that will get you in trouble with the law."

"Not if it's done right."

"Now you're really scaring me." Melissa squeezed his arm. "Those two are dangerous."

"They're not the only ones." Fargo had said enough. She pried for details but he was a clam. At the Filmore they parted. She had to work and he went to the bar and got a bottle and took it to a corner table. He wasn't in the mood for more company but he got some anyway, and it was wearing a tin star.

"William Mercer sent for me a while ago," Marshal Shicklin said. "He says you've been bothering him. He wants me to run you out of town."

Fargo opened the bottle and gulped and smacked the bottle down, spilling some. Welcome warmth spread through him, washing away a lot of the pain. "Try," he said.

Shicklin spread his hands, palms out. "I told him I needed a better reason."

Not that Fargo gave a damn but he asked, "What did Mercer say to that?"

"That he was disappointed. He hinted as how, come the next election, he might back someone else."

"And you're still not running me out?"

"Give me credit for some backbone. It helps that I know things about Mercer that would put *him* behind bars if word got around."

"I'm all ears."

Shicklin shook his head. "Give me credit for some brains, too. Secrets are like gold. A smart man hoards them until he needs them."

Fargo drank and stared out the window at the passersby.

"Miles Blackburn and his partner, Hitch."

"Oh, hell," Shicklin said.

"Where can I find them?"

"You don't want to."

Fargo drew his Colt and placed it on the table with a thump. Several patrons at nearby tables looked over.

"You're bluffing," Shicklin said. "You wouldn't put a bullet in a lawman. Not in broad daylight. Not with so many witnesses."

"Where?" Fargo said.

"I honestly don't know."

"You wouldn't know honest if it bit you on the ass." Fargo upended the bottle. Wiping his mouth with his sleeve, he said, "An arm or a leg would loosen your tongue."

"Maybe it would and maybe it wouldn't. But I'm telling the truth. Those two never stay in one place too long. Last week it was the Leadville Hotel. The week before that they were in Clear Creek on business. Before that they were houseguests of your favorite banker."

"Damn," Fargo said.

"They came to see you, didn't they? I'm surprised you're still breathing."

"Another body so soon after the boy was killed might stir people up. Questions would be asked. Mercer doesn't want that."

"You have no proof he's behind it."

"I don't need any."

Marshal Shicklin made a clucking sound. "Listen to yourself. Judge and jury. Kill him and you *will* hang."

"For now I want Blackburn and Hitch. I'll get around to Mercer later."

"Listen to you."

"I'm waiting."

"You're acting like God Almighty. But I'm being honest with you." Shicklin motioned at the street. "Oro City has half a dozen hotels. We have ten to twelve boardinghouses. There are apartments and homes for rent. They could be anywhere."

"You can find out."

"And then I have to clean up the mess you make or have the undertaker cart you off? No, thanks. You want them, you find them on your own." The lawman pushed back his chair and ambled out the batwings.

Fargo spent the next hour working on the bottle. He had a third of it to go when Melissa came over and pecked him on the cheek.

"I just wanted to let you know that I get off at midnight if you'd care for a second helping." She winked and grinned and started to walk off but he held on to her arm.

"Who's the best tailor in town?"

"Why do you want to know?"

"Answer the damn question."

"That's easy, though. It's Collandar, on Baker Street. He charges twice as much as everyone else but they say he's the best in the Rockies."

"He'll do," Fargo said.

The shop was nestled between a druggist and a shoemaker. A bell tinkled as Fargo entered. A mouse of a man, spectacles on the tip of his long nose, was perched on a stool, sewing. He looked up, saw Fargo and the bottle in Fargo's hand, and straightened.

"This isn't a saloon, sir."

"Are you Collandar?"

"I am. Who are you and why are you here? I can see by your attire that you favor deerskin. If it's new buckskins you need, the man to see is Harry Whittaker over by the feed and grain. He's old and his sight is going but his buckskins would make a redskin green with envy."

Fargo fingered a waistcoat on a wire frame. "You do good work."

"I should say I do. I've been a tailor for thirty-one years."

"Have a drink," Fargo said, and held out the Monongahela. "On me."

"No, thank you."

Fargo pushed the bottle against Collandar's chest. "I
wasn't asking."

"I'm working. I don't care for a drink. I hardly ever touch
hard spirits. They are the devil's juice."

"It's a trade," Fargo said.

"A what?"

"I'm letting you have a drink and you're returning the
favor by telling me where I can find Miles Blackburn."

"I've never heard of the man," Collandar said much too
quickly.

"You do his tailoring. When was the last time he was in?"

"I tell you I don't know him." Collandar went to climb
from the stool and Fargo stepped in front of him. "What on
earth are you doing? Out of my way."

"Ever been beaten into the ground?"

"What? No." Collandar drew back. He was perspiring
and his lower lip twitched.

"Ever been left to lie in the dirt?"

"No, I tell you."

"I have," Fargo said. He swallowed some whiskey. "Your
friend Blackburn and his friend Hitch gave me this goose
egg." He touched his head.

"I never said Mr. Blackburn is my friend."

"Ah. Then you do know him." Fargo offered the bottle
again. "Are you sure you don't want some?"

"Cut it out, will you? I'm a busy man. Go away or I shall
call the marshal."

Fargo sighed and set the bottle on the counter. Bending,
he palmed the Arkansas toothpick.

"What are you doing?"

"I keep it razor sharp." To demonstrate, Fargo selected a
spool of thread from several the tailor was using and sliced
off a few inches.

"Stabbing me won't get you the information," Collandar
said defiantly.

"You?" Fargo said, and moved to the waistcoat on the
wire frame. He touched the tip of the blade to the fabric.

71

"Be careful!" the tailor bleated. "That's a special order for an important customer. He needs it tomorrow for a wedding."

"Razor sharp," Fargo said again, and cut off a button.

Collandar shrieked and bounded off his stool. "Please. Stop. A button I can replace but do anything more—"

"Miles Blackburn."

Collandar wrung his hands. "You are most persistent—do you know that? Yes, I've done work for him."

"How recently?"

"About two weeks ago. I modified a dress coat. He's quite vain about his girth."

"Did he pick the coat up or have you deliver it?"

"He wanted me to take it over and—" Collandar stopped. "Damn you."

"What's the address?"

"I will only give it to you if you promise to be the soul of discretion."

"Write it down."

Moving behind the counter, the tailor opened a large account book. "Once you have it, I want you out of my shop. And never set foot in here again."

"You, sir, are a gentleman."

"And you, sir, are a son of a bitch."

"Yes," Fargo said. "I am."

13

The house was on a side street, set well back amid tall coni-
fers. The tailor had told Fargo that it was owned by a well-
to-do widow who rented out the upper floor. By Oro City
standards her rooms were luxurious.

Evening had spread shadows abroad when Fargo sta-
tioned himself behind an oak across the street. He would do
this right. There was bound to be gunplay and he didn't want
the old lady or anyone else hurt.

Time passed. Night shaded the grays to black and nearly
every building in Oro City lit with light.

Fargo had plenty of time. Brandy wouldn't be back from
Denver until morning. He'd promised to take the next run,
which wouldn't leave until two in the afternoon.

Down the street a dog yapped. Somewhere else a cat
meowed and went on meowing until someone yelled.

The front door opened and out came the widow. She wore
a nice dress and had her gray hair in a bun. She went to a
small table on her porch and lit a lamp and then she went
back in.

Presently she reappeared, carrying a tray with a china
teapot and a cup and saucer. She set the tray on the table
and took a seat. Filling a cup, she sat back and contentedly
sipped while gazing out over the city and up at the stars.

Fargo was debating whether to go talk to her when two
figures came up the street. He recognized one of their voices.

Miles Blackburn was as flawlessly dressed as ever. He
was going on about something to Hitch, who always seemed
to do more listening than talking.

Fargo ducked behind the oak.

". . . is so full of himself, it's all I can do not to laugh in his face," Blackburn was saying.

"He's paying us," Hitch said.

"Yes, I know. And we are consummate professionals. But still. The man has no breeding. All he cares about is power and money."

"One is the other," Hitch said.

"My, aren't you in a philosophical frame of mind?" Blackburn said. "But men like him still anger me. They're the reason so much is wrong with this world."

"Typical."

"Typical of him or typical of me?"

"His kind are ticks that suck on the blood of everyone else."

The pair came to the gate and Blackburn opened it. "Aptly put, my good fellow."

Fargo was set to step from behind the tree but a man and a woman came along the street from the other direction. By the time the pair had passed him, Blackburn and Hitch were on the porch with their landlady. Blackburn sat down to tea with her but Hitch went inside. Shortly after, a light came on in an upstairs window.

From where Blackburn sat, Fargo doubted Blackburn could see him. Moving quickly and staying on the opposite side of the street, he went to the next intersection, crossed, and made his way to the rear of the property. A short fence was no obstacle.

Steps brought him to the back door. He tried the latch. The door wasn't barred. Opening it a crack, he peered in. It was the kitchen. He listened and heard only the drone of voices from the front of the house and the click of a clock. Slipping inside, he closed the door and cat-footed to a hall. Stairs led to the second floor. Through a front window he saw Blackburn and the landlady. The window was open and he could hear her talking.

". . . agree that a double stitch is better." She tittered and declared, "Honestly, Mr. Blackburn, the things you know amaze me. Most men wouldn't have a clue."

"I am well versed in the domestic arts, madam."

"Yes, you are, more so than any man I've ever met." She patted his hand. "I hope you won't mind my saying this, but with your refined manners and your fondness for clothes, you would make a wonderful woman."

"Why, thank you, my dear."

Fargo palmed his Colt and went up the stairs. He tried to take them two at a stride but his wounded leg protested. He was afraid one of the stairs would creak; none did. Near the top he paused to listen. The second floor was quiet but Hitch was there somewhere. Cautiously, he climbed the last few steps. The hallway was empty.

Judging by the window that had glowed with light, Hitch was in the second door on the right. Fargo put his ear to it.

He detected no sound. Lightly placing his hand on the latch, he braced himself and flung the door wide, cocking the Colt as he did.

It was a bedroom, and no one was there.

Fargo entered, shut the door, and stood with his back to the wall. When the door opened he would be behind it. He was puzzled as to where Hitch had gotten to but it didn't much matter. If this was Hitch's bedroom, Hitch would return.

The latch scraped.

Fargo inwardly grinned at the surprise Hitch was in for. But he was the one surprised when the door swung in with brutal force and slammed against him. It caught him full in the face, and for a few moments he was dazed.

Then Hitch was in front of him. Hitch's right leg swept up and his foot caught Fargo on the jaw. Fargo tried to bring the Colt to bear but Hitch gripped his wrist and twisted and suddenly the Colt was in Hitch's hand, pointed at him.

Hitch stepped back.

Fargo shook his head to clear it. At any instant he expected the revolver to boom and to feel the hot rip of lead through his body.

Hitch just stood there, showing no emotion whatsoever. "You're wondering how," he said.

Fargo gauged the distance and didn't try.

"I went down for a glass of water and saw you slip in the back door," Hitch said. "I hid in the parlor and followed you up."

Fargo stared at his own Colt.

"It might be a while. He loves to talk and Mrs. Winslow adores him."

"Blackburn?" Fargo said.

"Who else?" Hitch backed to a chest of drawers and leaned against it and folded his arms. He was so sure of himself, he didn't bother to point the Colt. "How did you find us?"

Fargo didn't answer.

"You're only making it harder on yourself," Hitch said. "We'll find out once he comes up. We have ways of making people tell us things."

"I bet you do."

Hitch sighed. "I never rile. Insults have no effect. You can't provoke me into making a mistake. I never make mistakes."

"Modest, too."

A suggestion of a smile touched Hitch's thin lips. "You don't give up, do you?"

"Not so long as I'm breathing."

Hitch nodded. "I told him you were different. When we were hired to give you that message, we did some checking. We know more about you than anyone in Oro City."

"You think you do," Fargo said.

"Scout, guide, tracker, marksman, you've done it all," Hitch recited. "But you only work when you have to and then only so you'll have money for whiskey and women and cards."

"You did do some checking."

"We haven't lasted as long as we have by being careless. But I must say, we never expected you to find us."

"Then you do make mistakes."

"Our first," Hitch said.

"Your last," Fargo rejoined.

This time Hitch smiled. "I admire a man with confidence. But I'm afraid by tracking us down you've stepped over the line."

"Which line would that be?"

"The line between breathing and dead. We told you at the stable this was business and not personal. You should have let it drop."

"Would you have?"

Hitch was quiet a moment. "No," he admitted. "If someone did to me what we did to you, I'd find them and make them suffer until they begged me to stop, only I wouldn't stop."

"Then you shouldn't be surprised I came after you."

"You have more grit than most but by tracking us down you've become a threat and we can't have that."

"How many people have you and your partner killed?"

"We don't like to boast."

"How many?"

"Twenty-three. We've worked all over, from New York to New Orleans to the Rockies. We're the best at our line of work and we're paid a lot of money for our services."

"How many have you beat up?"

"I haven't counted them. I doubt Miles has, either. Were I to guess, I would say a couple of hundred." Hitch paused. "Why all these questions?"

Fargo shrugged. "Just killing time."

"And wondering why I haven't killed *you*, no doubt," Hitch said. "Mrs. Winslow would hear the shot and come up to investigate and then we'd have to kill her so she couldn't tell anyone, and Miles likes the old windbag."

"Damn considerate of you."

"I am always considerate when it comes to Miles."

Fargo bit off a reply.

"Besides, Miles will want to talk to you himself. Then the fun will begin."

"Fun?"

"The cutting and the breaking. I once kept a man alive for seventy-two hours after I'd cut off his fingers and his nose and stuck needles into his eyes and . . ." Hitch stopped. "It wasn't pretty."

"They never are," Fargo said.

"Every job has unsavory aspects."

"Who sent you to give me the message to leave town?"

"Our clients are confidential. Miles told you that. We never betray their trust."

"Was it William Mercer?"

"No."

"I don't believe you."

"Believe whatever you want," Hitch responded. "I can't tell you who it was but I can tell you who it wasn't and it wasn't Mercer."

"Blackburn and you have stayed at his house for a while."

Hitch grinned. "You've been checking around, too. And

it was only for a couple of days." He cocked his head as if listening. "Mercer wanted to hire us for a job and we told him we'd think about it."

Fargo had more to ask but footsteps came down the hall and Miles Blackburn entered, smiling.

"That landlady of ours is positively delightful. She just taught me a new stitch that—" Blackburn saw Fargo. "Well, well. What do have we here, Mr. Hitch?"

"A visitor."

"Tsk, tsk, Mr. Fargo. You would have been smart to leave well enough alone."

"I told you he wouldn't," Hitch said. "I told you this one is different."

"Rub it in." Blackburn smiled at Fargo. "Any last words, sir, before we end your earthly existence?"

14

With the blindfold on Fargo had to rely on his other senses. His hands were tied behind his back but his legs were free. He heard Miles Blackburn cough. Blackburn was leading the horse he was on. Behind them trailed Hitch.

Fargo's side was sore from where they had dropped him. They'd been spiriting him from the house by way of the kitchen door when Blackburn tripped, pitching him to the wood floor.

"Careful," Hitch had warned, "or your girlfriend will hear."

Blackburn had laughed mirthlessly. "Oh, that's a good one. I should ask her out to spite you."

Now, winding up a mountain in the starlit dead of night, Miles Blackburn twisted in his saddle. "I'm terribly sorry about the inconvenience but we couldn't very well kill you in our landlady's house, could we?"

"I could have done it quietly enough," Hitch said. "Knife or garrote or my bare hands."

"You can kill anyone, anywhere," Blackburn said.

"Then why didn't you let me?"

"There is a time and a place for everything, my dear Hitch."

"You just didn't want me to have to kill her. Yet you took her horse without asking."

"All we're doing is borrowing it. We'll take it back once this is done."

Fargo wished they would shut up so he wouldn't be distracted by their chatter. He was trying to figure out where they were. The scent of pine, the occasional prick of a limb, and the muffled thud of hooves on a carpet of pine needles told him they were in a forest. "How much farther?"

"Are you that eager to die?" Miles Blackburn asked.

"We're about a mile from Oro City, aren't we?" Fargo fished for clues.

"A mile north of it," Blackburn amended. "In about ten minutes we'll reach our destination."

"You shouldn't have told him that," Hitch said.

"What harm can it do?" Blackburn asked. "He's bound and helpless."

"A man like him is never helpless," Hitch said.

When Fargo first met them he'd been under the impression that Blackburn was the smart one but now he knew better. Hitch was smarter and sharper and that much more dangerous.

"Wouldn't it be fun to tell him who really hired us?" Miles Blackburn said.

"Don't joke about that," Hitch replied.

"Who's joking? I'd like to see the expression on his face. He'd never guess in a million years."

"We gave our word, Miles."

"He'd take the knowledge with him to his grave. Where's the harm?"

"The harm is in breaking our word."

"You can be tedious at times, Mr. Hitch," Blackburn said irritably. "You treat our profession as if it's some sort of holy crusade."

"When a man gives his word he should keep it."

"It depends on who he gives it to."

"No, Miles," Hitch said. "It doesn't."

Fargo agreed but he would be damned if he would say so. Clenching his teeth, he continued to rub his wrists back and forth as he had been doing since they threw him over the horse. In the dark Hitch hadn't seen what he was up to.

"How about if we tell him as we push him over the edge?" Blackburn proposed.

"Not even then."

It sounded to Fargo as if they were going to shove him over a cliff, maybe to make it seem like an accident if his body was ever found. Why they didn't just shoot him or slit his throat was a mystery. And a mistake. His wrists were raw and he had lost a lot of blood but he had done it—he was free.

"You lack dramatic flair," Miles Blackburn was criticizing his companion.

"And you could do with less of it."

"Drama is the spice of life, my dear fellow. Just ask Shakespeare."

"I can't," Hitch said. "He's dead."

Fargo turned his head and rubbed the blindfold against his shoulder. It moved but not enough. He rubbed again, harder. It still wouldn't budge. The knot was too tight.

"You have always worried too much," Blackburn went on. "Of your few faults, your worst is that you have never learned to relax and enjoy life."

"And yours is that you do not worry enough."

Fargo sensed that the horses were starting up a grade. He could still smell the pines but they wouldn't be in forest forever. If he was going to do something, he should get to it. Whipping his hands to his face, he tore at the blindfold. The damn thing still wouldn't come off.

"Miles!" Hitch yelled.

Suddenly Fargo could see. He dropped the blindfold and dived and crashed onto brush that cushioned his fall. A few quick rolls and vegetation closed around him.

"He's getting away!"

The undergrowth crackled. Fargo flattened and a horse went by. Seconds later another did on his other side.

"Where is he?" Blackburn hollered.

Fargo stayed still. He was invisible in the dark. They were reining right and left and Blackburn was swearing. So long as a horse didn't step on him he stood a chance. The hoofbeats drew away and he deemed it safe to rise. As quiet as an Apache, he moved in the opposite direction. In a dozen yards he emerged into a clearing.

A lean figure reared.

"Going somewhere?"

Fargo was impressed. Knowing that he would concentrate on their horses, Hitch had jumped off to search on foot. "Damned clever," he said.

"We can do this easy or hard," Hitch said.

Fargo crouched. He wished he had his Arkansas toothpick. They'd taken it from him when they tied him.

"Hard it is," Hitch said, and came at him in a rush.

Fargo got his arms up to protect his face and his belly. He forgot that Hitch preferred to use his feet. He was knocked back, his gut feeling as if it had been stomped by a mule. It was unsettling. He outweighed Hitch by fifty to sixty pounds. How could the man kick so hard?

Hitch didn't say anything. He flicked a fist with lightning speed and, when Fargo ducked, kicked him in the leg.

Fargo hadn't seen Hitch's foot move. He staggered and almost fell.

Skipping in, Hitch arced his right foot at Fargo's head. Fargo sidestepped, straight into a fistful of knuckles.

Again he retreated and bumped into a tree.

Hitch fell into a peculiar stance. He moved his hands in a strange pattern, his fingers rigid. Hitch's left arm darted out and Fargo blocked it. He didn't block the other. Pain shot from his neck to his toes and half his body went numb.

Fargo moved, with difficulty. Hitch sidled after him but didn't attack. He realized the beanpole was in no hurry to finish their fight. "You son of a bitch."

Hitch stopped.

"You're playing with me."

"I admit to a certain pleasure in doing so, yes."

Fargo was stalling. Sensation was returning but he needed another minute. "Where did you learn to fight like that?"

"Nippon."

"Never heard of it."

"You would know it as Japan," Hitch said. "I was with Commodore Perry and spent five years there as part of a trade delegation."

The name meant nothing to Fargo. He paid little attention to what went on in the rest of the world. "Is that where you met Blackburn?"

"Miles and I met upon my return. We have been the best of friends since."

"How nice for you." Fargo flexed his fingers and shifted his legs. Feeling had returned.

"Time to end this," Hitch said, and launched himself into the air.

Fargo had no warning. He tried to dodge and a foot clipped his back. New pain lanced his spine and it was all he could do to stay on his feet.

Hitch alighted as gracefully as a cat. Pivoting on the balls of his feet, he fell into another peculiar stance. "You make it too easy."

Loud crashing shattered the night. The undergrowth crackled and into the clearing rode Miles Blackburn. "Hitch! I thought I heard your voice."

The deadly beanpole turned.

Whirling, Fargo darted into the forest. He ran as fast as he could, his wounded leg protesting, until the crash of bushes and limbs warned him they were after him. Abruptly halting, he went prone.

For the next half an hour the pair hunted for him. Twice they came uncomfortably close. Once he spotted a thin silhouette. At last they drifted off.

Fargo stayed where he was. Hitch had outwitted him once. He wouldn't make the same mistake again. The minutes turned into an hour and the hour into two. Wolves howled and a mountain lion screeched. A bear roared and coyotes raised their voices.

Fargo fell asleep. To him the ground was the same as a bed. A pink band framed the horizon and birds were singing when he opened his eyes and sat up. He was stiff and sore but refreshed. Pushing upright, he yawned and stretched.

Confident that Hitch and Blackburn were long gone, Fargo bent his steps toward Oro City. He had a long walk ahead.

A timbered slope brought him to a meadow just as the sun rose. He was about to step from cover when he caught a whiff of smoke.

Fargo hunkered. Gray tendrils pinpointed the fire. The high grass prevented him from seeing who made it but the three horses picketed nearby were a clue. He swore under his breath. Blackburn and Hitch hadn't gone back. They'd made camp and would no doubt spend all day searching.

Fargo flattened. He must get past them now, before they were up and about. Pumping his elbows and crabbing with his knees, he crawled into the grass. It rustled but not loud enough for them to hear.

Fargo went faster. He was halfway to the other side when someone coughed. Stopping, he slowly rose to his knees.

Through the stems he saw a form huddled by the fire.

Miles Blackburn was filling a coffeepot with water from a canteen.

Fargo resumed crawling. Soon he reached the tree line and the cover of some oaks. Grinning at how he had outwitted them, he stood and went around a trunk.

"Going somewhere?" Hitch asked. He was leaning against a tree with his arms folded.

"Damn."

Hitch patted the oak. "I was up in one of these all night, watching and waiting."

"Hope you didn't get any sleep," Fargo said.

"I can go days without."

"Are you ready to tell me who hired you yet?"

"You are a tenacious son of a bitch," Hitch said.

"Do your worst." Fargo put his weight on his good leg and waited. When it happened it would happen fast.

"We are more alike than you'll admit." Hitch moved away from the tree and adopted another unusual stance. "Are you ready to die?"

15

Hitch slid one foot forward and then the other, as intent as a rattlesnake on prey it was about to strike.

Fargo backed away. With his hurt leg he couldn't move as quickly as he would like. Hitch, with his strange Japanese style of fighting, had an edge. Hell, even if his leg wasn't hurt, Hitch still had an edge.

They'd taken his Colt and his knife. But they hadn't taken his belt. Quickly, he unbuckled it and pulled it free. His gun belt would hold his pants up.

Hitch stopped. "What are you doing?"

Fargo gripped the belt so that the big buckle hung down near his knee and wrapped the other end around his hand several times. Gripping it tightly, he swung the belt over his head and then held it at his side.

"You're joking."

Fargo smiled.

"You're only delaying the inevitable."

"Prove it," Fargo said.

Hitch assumed a stance and slid his legs forward, his hands poised to slash or thrust.

Fargo flicked his belt at the killer's face.

Hitch blocked it. The buckle struck the back of his hand and Hitch winced and stepped back. He looked at the drops of blood, betraying surprise.

"I'll take out an eye next," Fargo said.

Hitch dropped into a wide crouch. "You are resourceful, I will give you that. And you have uncommon luck. But your luck has run out and your pitiful excuse for a weapon will not save you."

"Prove it," Fargo said again.

Hitch sprang and Fargo swung. The heavy buckle sizzled the air and caught Hitch across the arm. Hitch tried to grab it but Fargo yanked and swung again, this time at Hitch's leg.

The *crack* of the buckle striking Hitch's knee was like the crack of a gunshot. Fargo sidestepped, keeping the belt in motion and not letting Hitch get closer.

Hitch was in pain. He was trying not to show it but the set of his jaw gave him away.

"Pitiful, huh?" Fargo taunted.

Hitch charged and Fargo retreated, swinging as he went. He had to be careful of the oaks. He swung at Hitch's face and Hitch raised his forearms to protect his eyes.

Fargo swung faster and harder, raining blow after blow. Hitch grabbed at the belt and in doing so exposed a cheek. Fargo lashed and backpedaled.

Hitch touched his cheek and stared at the blood on his fingertips. "I have underestimated you badly."

Fargo had another trick up his sleeve, and he used it now. He took a step back and gave a low cry and dropped to give the impression his wounded leg had buckled on him. He came down on his good knee and put his left hand on the ground as if to brace himself and dug his fingers into the soil.

"Your body betrays you."

Fargo pretended to be in too much pain to reply.

"Time to end this," Hitch said, and flew at him in a long bound.

Fargo was ready. He threw the dirt at Hitch's face and Hitch instinctively raised his hands and Fargo lashed the belt at Hitch's legs. It wrapped around Hitch's ankle. Fargo pulled, sweeping Hitch's leg out from under him. Hitch glanced down, startled. And then Hitch was on his back on the ground and bending to unwrap the belt but Fargo was already in motion. Keeping the belt taut, he kicked Hitch in the knee. Hitch twisted and kicked at his legs but Fargo jumped high into the air and came down with his knees bent. He smashed onto Hitch's chest and took a hand chop to his ribs that hurt abominably but didn't stop him. He rammed a fist to Hitch's jaw. Hitch chopped and he rammed another. He still had hold of the belt and Hitch's leg was bent up into the air. Hitch bucked but Fargo was too heavy for him. Hitch speared his fingers at Fargo's neck and Fargo felt the worst pain yet but it didn't slow him or stop him from slamming his fist again and again and again.

Suddenly Fargo realized Hitch wasn't moving. In a daze of pain, he stopped hitting him. Hitch's lips were pulp and his mouth a pool of blood. One cheek resembled mashed meat and one eyebrow was split.

Fargo sank onto his side. God, he hurt. He managed to sit up and checked Hitch for weapons. All he found was his toothpick, wedged under Hitch's belt. He pressed the tip to Hitch's throat. Hitch's killing days were about over.

"Mr. Hitch, where are you?"

Fargo looked up.

Miles Blackburn was coming through the oaks, looking all around, and he had a rifle.

Any moment Blackburn would spot him.

Dropping flat, Fargo crawled to a thicket and around it to the other side. He rose but stayed low. Inspiration struck, and he let out a loud groan.

"Hitch?"

Fargo heard heavy footsteps and a bleat of shock and horror.

"Hitch! My God! No!"

Backing away until it was safe, Fargo turned and hobbled as fast as he could toward their campfire. He glanced over a shoulder and saw Blackburn on his knees trying to revive Hitch and wiping his face with a handkerchief.

The fire had burned low. A log had been dragged near it for a seat. All three horses were hobbled. Fargo strapped on his belt, bent, and removed a hobble. Their saddlebags caught his eye. In the first one he opened he found his Colt. Grinning, he patted it, checked that there were five pills in the wheel, and twirled it into his holster. He also found an expensive leather wallet with four hundred and sixty-seven dollars. He crammed the money into his poke and tossed the wallet in the fire. The next saddlebag contained even more money— seven hundred and twenty. He added the money to his poke. "Thank you, gents," he said out loud.

Fargo removed the other hobbles. He slipped bridles on all three horses but saddled only the one. Climbing on, he led the other two to the west for a few hundred yards and then reined to the south.

Blackburn and Hitch had a long walk ahead.

Fargo wished he could see their faces when they returned to their camp. He laughed, then sobered. They would come after him. Hitch, in particular, wouldn't rest until he was dead.

Little did they know that he wouldn't until they were.

About ten in the morning he reached Oro City and rode straight to the Colorado Stage Company office. The stage was parked in front. Voices came from the office. He went in without knocking.

Brandy was at her desk. Rafer and another man on crutches were arguing with her. At the sight of him, she squealed his name and came around the desk and gripped him by the arms. "Skye. Thank heavens. No one could find you. I was beginning to think you'd run out on me and one of us would have to take the Denver stage and—" She stopped and her eyes narrowed. "What in God's name? You have a bruise on your neck and another on your face. Have you been in a fight?"

"You could call it that."

"Marshal Shicklin was here lookin' for you," Rafer said. "He was mad that I didn't know where you were."

"Let him look," Fargo said.

"That's not all," Rafer said. "Gil Whitten and Big Jim Buchanan were here askin' about you, too." He grinned. "You're right popular."

"They say what they wanted?"

Rafer shook his head. "Whitten said it was important he talk to you but he wouldn't say why."

Brandy was still staring at the bruises. "Are you fit enough to handle a stage?"

"More than," Fargo said, and flexed his wounded leg to demonstrate. It hurt but nowhere near as much as it did just two days ago.

"Thank God. Because if you hadn't shown up I was going to take it myself."

"Like hell," Rafer said. "You just got back and haven't had any sleep."

"And it's twenty hours or more there," the other man mentioned.

"I can go without sleep if I have to," Brandy said.

"Not for four days," Rafer said. "Not and handle a stage proper."

"Drop it," Brandy said. "Skye is here, so everything is fine." She sat on the edge of her desk. "And the other good news is that no one tried to rob me this time."

"Maybe they're afraid of tanglin' with him again," Rafer said with a bob of his stubble at Fargo.

"Do you need some sleep?" Brandy asked.

"No," Fargo replied. But he could use coffee. He stepped to the stove in the corner where a pot was always brewing and helped himself. He didn't bother with cream and sugar. He drank it black in thirsty gulps.

"You haven't told us who hit you," Brandy said.

"It's my problem."

"You need help, you say the word," Rafer said. "I'm not much of a shot but with a scattergun at close range I don't need to be."

"I'll let you know." Fargo set down the cup and went out and over to the stable. The Ovaro was in the stall, dozing. He patted it and the stallion nuzzled him. Stepping to the oat bin, he was about to fill a bucket when two shadows spread down the aisle. He spun, thinking it was Hitch and Blackburn, and swooped his hand to his Colt. But he didn't draw. "You two," he said.

"Us," Gil Whitten said. "We've been searching all over town for you." Behind him, Big Jim Buchanan nodded in greeting.

"What for?"

Whitten said something to the big Texan and Buchanan moved to the wide door and stood blocking the entrance.

"Expecting trouble?"

"There was another attempt on my life last night," Whitten said, leaning on his cane. "A shot in the dark that damn near put me in my grave."

"Did you see the shooter?"

Whitten scowled. "Not so much as a glimpse, I'm afraid. It came from behind the general store. Big Jim and I looked but the assassin had run off."

"Any ideas?"

"Marshal Shicklin is of the opinion that it could have been you."

"So that's why he was here asking for me."

"For what it's worth, I don't believe him," Whitten said. "You weren't in Oro City when the last two attempts were made."

"Is that what you came to tell me?"

"No. I understand you're to take the next stage to Denver. I'd like to have Big Jim go with you. He has an errand to run for me."

"What's wrong with your own stage?" Fargo said. The Cobb and Whitten line made regular runs to Denver, too.

"I'm being constantly watched. I'm sure of it. If he takes one of our stages, they'll see and perhaps wonder why I've sent him to Denver. I'm hoping that by taking your stage, they won't notice."

It seemed thin to Fargo but all he said was, "You'll be without a bodyguard until he gets back."

"I'm not defenseless, and I'll stay in my office until he returns." Whitten glanced at the big Texan. "His errand may solve this whole mystery."

"I don't suppose you'd care to tell me what you're up to?"

"No, I'm sorry. Not a word until I'm sure."

"Hell," Fargo said.

16

A good team knew the stage route as well as the driver. The horses had been over it so many times they could follow it in the dark of night with no difficulty.

A good driver used his whip sparingly and his brains a lot. He memorized the sharpest bends and steepest grades and knew when to goad the team and when to let them have their head.

The whip Brandy lent Fargo had a hickory handle, painted pink, and silver curlicues. As he hopped onto the front wheel rim and climbed from there to the box, Rafer chuckled.

"Don't let any of the drivers for other lines see you or they'll laugh you silly."

In addition to Big Jim Buchanan there were four other passengers. Two were townsmen, one looked to be a farmer, and the last was a middle-aged dumpling of a woman who glared at any man who came near her.

Fargo didn't invite anyone up on the box. It was considered an honor for a passenger to be asked but he had no interest in having company.

It was ten minutes to ten and they were set to pull out when the last person Fargo expected to see showed up at the office with her bag: Melissa Hart, in a red dress and matching bonnet.

Fargo was even more surprised when, after purchasing a ticket and having her bag stowed by Rafer in the rear boot, Melissa proceeded to come to the front and started to climb up beside him.

"Hold on. What do you think you're doing?"

Melissa smiled sweetly. "What does it look like? I'm riding up with you." Something in his expression gave her pause.

"Why? Don't you want me to? After we . . . I mean . . . I took it for granted. Can I or can't I?"

"It's not safe."

"No one will shoot a woman," Melissa said confidently. "They'd be strung up so fast their head would swim." She clambered up and perched beside him and fluffed her dress and her hair. "There. Won't this be fun?"

"It's a long ride," Fargo pointed out. "You could get rained on."

"A few raindrops never hurt anybody."

That reminded him. "You were just to Denver to fetch your grandmother and now you have to go back?"

Melissa nodded. "Not that it's any of your business but I'm having a dress made and I want to pick it up."

"They could send it to you."

"And what if the dress doesn't fit? I'll have to send it back and they'll make alterations and send it back to me. That could go on for weeks. No, experience has taught me it's best to try a dress on before it ever goes out the door." Melissa folded her hands in her lap. "Besides, I happen to like Denver. And it will be nice to get away from my grandma for a while."

"I thought you two were close."

"We are. She tends to prattle on, though, to where I am fit to scream."

Brandy came out of the office and frowned at Melissa. "We don't usually let women ride on the box."

"I'll be fine," Melissa said.

"It's not your decision. It's the driver's." Brandy looked at Fargo. "Say the word and she'll have to ride inside with the rest."

"Not if I don't want to, I won't."

"Yes," Brandy said. "You will."

"She can stay up here with me," Fargo said.

Melissa beamed.

"You might want to reconsider," Brandy told her. "You'll get flies and moths on your clothes. One or two might even get in your mouth."

"I've tasted worse things than bugs."

"The wind will make a mess of your hair," Brandy predicted. "It'll be tangled for a month of Sundays."

"My bonnet will protect me."

Brandy clearly wasn't happy. "I own this line. I could forbid you to ride up there."

"But you won't," Melissa said, "or I'll tell everyone how bossy you are and from here on out I'll only ever use the Cobb and Whitten stage line."

Brandy focused her anger on Fargo. "You better not let her distract you. Crash my stage and you'll answer to me."

"I'll make it back in one piece."

"You better." Brandy marched inside.

"Goodness," Melissa said. "Who put a burr up her petticoats?"

A light crack of the whip and they were under way. People and riders in the way moved aside. As they passed the Filmore House, Gil Whitten raised a hand to Fargo but seemed to stiffen when he saw Melissa. They came to the far end of the street.

Ahead stretched the winding road bounded by thick woodland.

The sun was warm on Fargo's face. He tasted the first of what would be miles of dust. He smelled the coach and the horses, and perfume. Under him the stage swayed like a baby's cradle.

"Isn't it gorgeous?" Melissa said with a sweep of her slender arm at the scenery.

"The mountains aren't the only thing that is," Fargo said, giving her a pointed look. Her perfume had stirred a notion.

"Behave," Melissa scolded. "We're not going to do it on top of a stage, and certainly not while the stage is moving, and double certainly not when we could go over a cliff or crash into a tree."

"Be fun to try."

Melissa glanced at him, and laughed. "You honestly would, wouldn't you?"

"Once it's dark," Fargo said.

"No, no, and no," Melissa said. "I have done some crazy things in my time but I draw the line at suicide."

"I can think of worse ways to die."

"I'd imagine there are a hundred of them," Melissa agreed. "But the answer is still no."

"Maybe I can change your mind."

"And maybe these horses will sprout wings and fly."

For a mile the road was flat. Then they came to the first grade that led into a series of switchbacks. Fargo had his hands full until they reached the bottom.

Melissa hummed and gazed in delight at the high peaks capped with snow and at a pair of bald eagles soaring on outstretched wings. "Isn't this marvelous? I've never gotten to sit on the box before."

"You can take the reins if you want." Fargo didn't mean it.

Laughing, Melissa shook her head. "I'd wreck us, sure as anything. Believe me when I say I'm in awe of men like Rafer, and yes, like you. How you manage is beyond me. Once Rafer took us through a dust storm where I couldn't see my hand in front of my face. And do you know what he said when I asked him how he did it?" She didn't wait for Fargo to answer. "He told me that he smelled his way through. Can you do that?"

"No." Fargo would be the first to admit he wasn't as experienced or as skilled as men like Rafer. But then, men like Rafer weren't as experienced or as skilled at tracking as he was. Or living off the land. Or dealing with Indians. Or killing.

"I've heard of a woman who works as a driver," Melissa mentioned. "She dresses like a man and no one can tell the difference."

Fargo had met her but didn't say so.

"I admire women like that. Women who can make it on their own. Women who don't need a man to feel complete."

"You liked being with a man two nights ago."

"Men have their uses and that's one of them. But there are times when I could go a whole month without a man and be as happy as can be." Melissa bit her lower lip. "Some men are poison. A girl knows she shouldn't fall for them but she does, and the next she knows, she's up to her neck in trouble."

"That works both ways."

"True. It's a pity, isn't it? Love should be easy on the heart and on the nerves."

"What the hell are we talking about?"

Melissa laughed. "Nothing. Wishful thinking, I suppose. A girl can always dream."

Fargo concentrated on a sharp turn. The team swept in and

around without the stage rocking. They were well trained, these horses.

"May I ask you a question?"

Fargo regretted letting her join him. He should have known she would talk his ear off. "What else do we have to do."

"I'll take that as a yes." Melissa shifted toward him. "I've heard you were warned to leave town. Is that true?"

"Where did you hear that?"

"Someone at the saloon," Melissa said. "I can't remember his name."

"There's a surprise," Fargo said. "But yes, I was warned."

"Why didn't you go?"

"You want me to tuck tail?" Fargo wouldn't last out the year if word got around he had turned yellow. He had enemies.

"It's the smart thing to do. You don't have a stake in this silly stage war."

"Silly?" Fargo said.

"What else would you call it? There are enough customers for two stage lines but someone has to be the one and only. It's all about the money." Melissa sighed. "Greed is like a disease. Once you catch it, it can damn near destroy you."

"Brandy's not the greedy one," Fargo said.

"She's not sensible, either, that woman. She's lost her husband and most of her drivers and almost all her stages are in no shape to use, yet she refuses to give up. I would if I was her. I'd sell out in a minute. It's just not worth it."

"Brandy has her pride."

"Is that all it is? Pride will be her downfall, then. And when she's gone under, what will she have to show for her trouble? A patch of dirt with her rotting bones. That's all."

Fargo took his eyes from the road. "I thought you just said you admire women who try to make it on their own?"

Melissa averted her face. "I do. But this is different. Brandy is just being stubborn."

After that she didn't utter a word for over an hour.

Fargo was glad to be left to his driving. In his mind's eye he pictured the large map that hung on the office wall with the route plainly laid out. He'd memorized it so that switchbacks and turns didn't catch him unawares.

There were four relay stations between Oro City and Denver.

At each they would change teams and the passengers could have food and drink.

The first was called Higgins Station after the couple who ran it. It consisted of a log building, a large corral for horses, a couple of sheds, and an outhouse.

In a swirl of dust Fargo brought the stage to a stop. Higgins and his missus were waiting. Higgins had a helper, a Mexican, and they tended to the horses while Fargo walked about stretching his legs.

Someone else had the same idea.

"We're makin' good time," Big Jim Buchanan said.

Fargo grunted.

"It might be best if you let me ride on top with you over the next leg instead of that pretty gal."

Fargo put his hand to the small of his back and arched his spine. "Why is that?"

"Because," the Texan said, "we're bein' followed."

17

Fargo took a seat at one end of a long table, facing the door. Mrs. Higgins brought him a pot of coffee and filled his cup. He wasn't all that hungry but he ate a small meal anyway. Mr. Higgins had shot a buck that morning and there was venison, potatoes, and string beans.

Big Jim Buchanan sat on his left, also facing the door, his tree-trunk arms folded across his broad chest. "I saw a flash of metal or a spyglass," he was explaining. "Not once but four times. I'm surprised you didn't see it, too."

Fargo was embarrassed to admit that he hadn't once looked behind them since leaving Oro City. "I'll be on the lookout from here on out."

Big Jim gazed at Melissa, who had joined the other passengers and was gaily laughing and talking. "She sure is a pretty filly."

"A lot of women are pretty," Fargo said, spearing a piece of deer meat with his fork.

"A lot of women are sidewinders. A lot of men, too."

"That supposed to mean something?"

"Just that when I was totin' a badge, I learned never to trust anyone, no matter how pretty they are."

"What are you getting at?"

"Nothin'."

Fargo had the sense that the big Texan was holding something back. "You ever going to say why Whitten has sent you to Denver?"

"He thinks he knows who is behind this whole mess. I'm to dig around for him and find out if he's right."

"Why doesn't he do his own digging?"

"It might make the ones behind it suspect he is onto them."

"Them?" Fargo said. "As in two or three or ten?"

"All you need to know right now is what I've already told you. Don't trust anyone."

"Does that include you?"

The Texan grinned.

"I don't like it that Whitten is keeping everything so close to his vest," Fargo said sourly. "I have as much stake in this as he does."

"Hardly. His company might go under if these varmints have their way. What do you have a stake?"

"My life."

"Well, there's that," Buchanan conceded, and chuckled.

"At least give me a hint."

"You're startin' to sound like a gal I lived with down to Dallas. She could nag a man to death without half tryin'."

"Damn it."

"Sorry, but I'm loyal to whoever hires me and at the moment I work for Gil Whitten."

Higgins came over. He was a short, balding man in his forties who wore overalls and a floppy hat. "Excuse me, gents," he said. "I have something to say to the driver, here."

"Say it," Fargo said with his mouth full.

Higgins leaned on the table. "I don't think it's much but the missus says it might be important and for me to tell you."

"I'm still listening," Fargo said.

"About an hour before you got here, me and her were inside. She was fixing supper and I was mending a harness." Higgins paused. "We heard riders go by."

About to spear a slice of potato, Fargo looked at him. "The station is next to a road."

"True," Higgins said, and coughed. "Riders go by all the time. A lot of them stop to water their horses or to jaw some. These didn't."

Fargo was puzzled. "And that's so unusual you thought you should mention it?"

"No, sir," Higgins said. "It wasn't unusual that they didn't stop. But it was that they were pushing their horses so hard. It's a long way to Denver. As fast as they were going, they'll wear out their animals long before they get there." He fiddled with a button on his shirt. "And there was something else."

The man didn't go on, and finally Fargo said, "Are you waiting for Christmas?"

"Oh. Sorry. It's just that I'm used to the missus telling me when I can finish what I'm saying."

Big Jim Buchanan laughed. "She tell you what clothes you should wear, too?"

"As a matter of fact, she does."

"Oh," Buchanan said.

Fargo drummed his fingers on the table. "Higgins, if you don't get to the goddamn point, so help me I'll hit you over the head with this plate."

"Don't, please. She'd be mad at me for breaking her dishes."

"And some people wonder why I've never gotten hitched," Fargo said.

"Sorry?"

"The riders, Higgins. What about those riders?"

"Well, it's just that I happened to be sitting by the door and we had it open to let in air. I looked out and saw them ride by. And as they went past they all looked away."

"Away from what?" Buchanan asked.

"Why, from the station. It was peculiar, almost as if they didn't want anyone to see their faces."

"Thanks for letting me know." Fargo thought that was the end of it and speared a string bean.

"I didn't get a good look at them but I did notice the one who was out in front. He was all in black."

Fargo froze. "Black, you say?"

"Yes, sir. He must be awful fond of it. He had one of those black hats with a wide brim and he was wearing a black duster and black boots."

Fargo's leg started to hurt.

"I didn't know if it was important or not but the missus reckoned you should know."

"She did right."

"She usually does." Higgins smiled and left them.

Buchanan stared at Fargo. "What's the matter? You look like somebody just walked over your grave."

Fargo chewed on the green bean but he'd lost his appetite. "The gent who put lead into my leg wore a black duster."

"You think they're the stage robbers?"

"I wouldn't bet they're not," Fargo said.

"Them in front of us and someone trailin' behind." Buchanan grinned. "We could swap lead before too long."

"Don't sound so happy about it." Fargo wasn't. He had the passengers to think of. He got up and went out and over to the stage. He walked slowly around it and acted as if he was inspecting the wheels and the thoroughbraces but the whole time he surreptitiously scanned the slopes above the station. At length he was rewarded with a gleam of light. "Now who can that be?"

"What did you say, Skye?" Melissa came around the stage, her face and hair and dress as fresh as when they started out from Oro City.

"I was talking to myself," Fargo said.

"I do that all the time." Smiling happily, she gazed up and down the road. "I do so love these trips. I love anything that gets me out of the saloon for a while."

"You don't like your work?"

"What's to like about being groped? What's to like about putting up with drunks? What's to like about having to go to bed with a man when I might not want to?"

The Filmore House was high class. Fargo wasn't aware the owner made the girls do that. He said as much.

"Well, no, not there," Melissa replied. "But other saloons I've worked at." She raised her arms toward the box. "Why don't you give me a boost? I'll sit up there until we leave."

"No," Fargo said.

"I beg your pardon."

"Someone else is riding with me the next leg. You ride inside with the rest."

Melissa looked hurt. "I thought we were friends."

"It's company policy that the passengers take turns," Fargo lied. As with most stage lines, it was up to the driver whether anyone rode on the box or not.

Melissa came close and placed her hand on his chest and bestowed her sweetest smile. "I deserve special treatment, don't you think?"

"Brandy Randall wouldn't like it."

"She doesn't ever have to know." Melissa caressed his cheek. "What do you say?"

"It's still no."

"I *need* to be up there with you." Melissa gripped the front of his shirt. "Please."

"Don't do this."

Melissa pressed her body against his. "You wanted to have me again, didn't you? Let me on the box and we will. I promise."

"You said it was loco."

"I was teasing," Melissa said. "I want to as much as you want me." She raised her arms again. "Give me that boost and I am all yours later."

"Can't," Fargo said, reluctantly.

Melissa grew red and smacked him so hard, it was a wonder she didn't break her hand. Wheeling, she strode into the station, her body flouncing with every step.

Fargo used his tongue to make sure none of his teeth was loose.

Around the other side of the stage sauntered Big Jim Buchanan, his thumbs in his gun belt. "I couldn't help but overhear. I'll ride inside if you'd rather have your fun."

"I need your gun more than a screw."

Buchanan's eyes crinkled with humor. "Few gents would turn down a gal as pretty as her. You must be part Texan."

"Texans don't fancy women?"

"We fancy the hell out of females," Buchanan said. "But there is more to life than pokin' them."

Fargo liked him more and more.

It was another ten minutes before they left. Higgins came out and informed Fargo that one of the horses was new to the ribbons.

"He's on the off wheel so he shouldn't give you much trouble."

"I'll keep an eye on him," Fargo replied. Stage companies didn't stick just any old horse on a tongue. The animals were carefully chosen and carefully trained. In flat country four horses were usually enough but in mountainous terrain, with so many steep grades and turns, six were needed. The two at the front were called the leaders. They were always the most sure-footed and weren't prone to spook. In the middle were the swing pair. They had to have good balance and respond well to the leaders. Closest to the stage were the wheelers. They were the strongest, with the most pulling power.

Higgins called the passengers out. "Time's up, ladies and gents. If you're going on, get on."

Fargo climbed onto the box and unwrapped the ribbons from the brake handle.

The stage tilted, and Big Jim Buchanan was beside him. "Haven't ridden on one of these in a while," he remarked. "I forgot these seats aren't made for a man my size."

Melissa came out and crossed to the stage and Higgins gave her a hand in. She didn't so much as glance at the box.

"I reckon you're not her favorite person right about now," Buchanan said.

"I'll live."

"You're awful optimistic."

The door slammed and Higgins thumped the stage and called up, "All loaded."

Fargo raised the ribbons.

"Have a safe trip," Higgins hollered.

"I sure as hell hope so," Fargo said.

18

The next leg was a twisting snake of bends and grades.

Fargo devoted his full attention to the team. Fortunately Buchanan was there to do what he couldn't—keep an eye out for trouble.

The big Texan broke open the shotgun Fargo had passed to him. "It's already loaded," he said. He snapped it shut and cradled it.

The sun was sinking to the west and the shadows were lengthening. Patches of the road were often in premature darkness.

Fargo was glad to have the sun at his back and not in his face. He negotiated a turn, the leaders and the swing horses and the wheelers responding to the ribbons as if they were puppets on strings. He sat back, grateful for another straight stretch.

"They'll wait until it's dark," Buchanan guessed. "So they can get close without us spottin' them."

"Works out better for us," Fargo said. "It's harder for them to hit what they can't see."

"They hit you."

"Ouch," Fargo said.

The Texan patted the shotgun. "They don't know we're ready for them. We'll have the edge."

"We hope." Fargo was saying that last word a lot lately.

"If they come at us from the front I'll clear a way with the cannon."

"They'll be hard to hit, even with that."

"Their animals won't."

Fargo glanced at him. A lot of men, and he was one of them, had a high regard for horses. He could no more shoot one than he could, say, a nun. "You can do that?"

"If I have to."

"Too bad we won't hear them until they're on us," Fargo said. The pounding of the team and the clatter of the stage would drown out the sound of their approach.

"Unless they're shootin'."

"There's that," Fargo said.

Buchanan twisted around and stayed that way for a while. Presently he faced front.

"Anything?" Fargo asked.

"If he's still back there he's stayin' hid."

"Or they are."

"Now I know how the turkeys in a turkey shoot feel."

A series of grades required Fargo's attention. By his reckoning they were about midway between Higgins Station and the next. Arklin Station, it was called.

A raven took wing and flew over their heads. Several does bounded off with tails high. A skunk was nosing around a stump and fled.

"Thank God," Buchanan said.

Fargo grinned. A stage that ran over one would stink for days.

The steepest slope yet unfolded below. Fargo judiciously applied the brake to slow the horses and to give him more tension in the lines.

"You're good at this."

At the bottom the road narrowed. Trees grew up to the edge, their limbs creating a pool of shadow as black as pitch.

Buchanan thumbed back the twin hammers on the shotgun. "Could be," he said.

Fargo tensed. They were moving slowly. They *had* to go slow on account of the grade. He tried to watch the woods and the horses, both. It made more sense for the robbers to wait for full dark but this was a good spot.

The stage was almost to the bottom. Fargo dared a glance at the trees and thought he saw movement. "Something on this side."

"This side, too."

"Hell," Fargo said, and lashed the team. The coach gave a sharp jolt. Inside, someone cried out.

Shots exploded. Riders appeared, shooting and shouting for them to stop.

Fargo used his whip. The leaders surged and the swing and wheel horses followed suit. The road ran straight for a quarter of mile, and they could fly.

Riders burst from the trees, three on the left and two on the right. All had bandannas over the lower half of their faces and their hats pulled low. Pistols cracked and smoked.

Fargo went faster.

"Stop, damn you!" a robber bawled, and reining in close, he took aim.

Buchanan cut loose. The man's head exploded like a pumpkin, leaving a stump that pumped blood, and the body pitched from the saddle.

Lead smacked the coach. Lead zinged off the rail. Lead struck the box.

Holding the ribbons and the whip in his left hand, Fargo palmed his Colt and banged two shots. A man toppled. Jamming the six-shooter in his holster, he resorted to the whip again.

The four remaining robbers weren't discouraged at all. They had fallen behind but they would easily catch up when the stage reached the next bend.

Turning in the seat, Buchanan brought the shotgun to his shoulder. He fired over the top of the stage and a horse squealed and crashed down.

Now there were three.

Something plucked at Fargo's hat.

Someone in the stage poked a hand out holding a pocket pistol and joined the fight.

Buchanan was reloading. "On my side!"

A rider had swept around from the rear: the man in the wide-brimmed black hat and black duster.

Fargo drew again and twisted but he didn't have a clear shot. The big Texan was in his way. "Get down!"

Buchanan started to duck.

The man in black was next to the stage. In swift succession he fired three times.

Grunting, Buchanan doubled over and almost dropped the shotgun. "I'm hit."

Fargo pointed his Colt at the rider in black and the man veered away. Again Fargo shoved the Colt into his holster and cracked his whip. For the next minute all was bedlam: the thunder of the team, shouts of panic from in the stage, more shots from those after them. As a bend swept toward them, the shots faded. Fargo glanced over his shoulder.

The man in black and the other two had turned back.

The stage roared around the curve. The coach tilted and a woman screamed as Fargo struggled to keep control. He hauled on the ribbons and pressed his boot to the brake and the coach righted itself. Another fifty yards and he brought it to a stop.

Buchanan had his big hands to his chest and his eyes were closed.

"How bad is it?" Fargo asked, putting a hand to the Texan's shoulder.

"See to the others."

Fargo swung down. From inside came weeping. Fearing the worst, he opened the door. "Is anyone hurt?"

The middle-aged dumpling was the one crying. She was a disheveled mess but she hadn't been shot. Melissa's bonnet hung lopsided over one ear and she was swearing as lively as a river rat. The farmer was pressed into a corner, his eyes as wide as saucers.

One of the townsmen was curled on the floor, his eyes empty of life, the pocket pistol beside him.

"He tried to help you," the dumpling squalled, "and that one in black shot him."

"Anyone else take a slug?" Fargo asked.

Several of them shook their heads.

The dumpling looked down at herself and groped her bosom. "I don't appear to be shot, no."

"All of you out," Fargo said, motioning.

"Is it safe?" the farmer asked.

"Are the outlaws gone?" the dumpling squeaked.

"Now," Fargo snapped, and grabbing her wrist, he hauled her out.

She squawked and slapped his arm. "The nerve of some people. You had no right to do that."

"The rest of you," Fargo commanded. When they had

complied, he slid his arms under the body and set it on the ground. He sought a bullet hole and found it. The slug had caught the man between the shoulder blades and pierced his heart.

Fargo stood and got one of the blankets the stage company furnished to ward off the night chill. He spread it flat, beckoned at the farmer and the other man, and together they placed the body on it and he folded the blanket over.

"Thank goodness," the dumpling said. "I couldn't bear to look at his face."

Only then did it occur to Fargo that Big Jim Buchanan hadn't climbed down from the box. He stepped onto the front wheel and said, "Why are you still up here?"

The Texan looked up. His hands, still pressed to his chest, were wet with blood. So was a good part of his shirt.

"Why didn't you tell me?" Fargo got an arm under him but it was like trying to lift a bull. He barked at the farmer and the townsman to help. They got Buchanan down and placed him on another blanket.

The Texan was paste-white and clammy with sweat.

Fargo knelt and pried at the big man's fingers. "Let me have a look."

"Lord, no," the dumpling said.

The exit wound was a few inches above Buchanan's sternum. The entry hole was under his right arm. As near as Fargo could tell, the slug had been deflected by a rib and torn from side to front. "Damn."

The Texan opened his eyes. "I'm done for, aren't I?"

Fargo's expression said it all.

"I always knew I wouldn't die in bed but I never reckoned on goin' like this." Buchanan sucked in a breath. "It was the hombre in black."

"I know," Fargo said.

"Do me a favor?" Buchanan coughed. "Hunt him down and blow out his wick."

"Count on it."

"I'm glad we met. I'd heard of you but always figured the newspapers made you out to be more than you are." Buchanan did more coughing. "But you're the real article. You'd do to ride the river with."

"Less talk," Fargo said. "You'll last longer."

"There's somethin' I've got to tell you. Remember me sayin' that Whitten thinks he knows who is behind this? He sent me to Denver to rustle up some information. Now it will have to be you who does the diggin'."

"Who does Whitten think it is?"

Buchanan didn't seem to hear him. "Go to the *Rocky Mountain News*. They keep a file of old stories. Ask them to look up—" He stopped.

"Look up what?" Fargo prompted. When he didn't get an answer he quickly felt for a pulse. There wasn't any.

"Is he—?" the dumpling said.

"What do you think?" Fargo roughly retorted. He swore and stood and kicked the ground.

"That won't help any," the dumpling said.

Fargo glared and she took a step back.

"What do we do now?" the farmer asked.

"We keep going."

"But what if they come after us? You'll be up there all alone."

"Don't remind me," Fargo said.

19

The stage rattled and creaked. Above, stars sparkled. The horses had calmed down and settled into the routine of the road.

Perched on the box, Fargo used the ribbons mechanically. He was deep in thought. He'd liked Big Jim Buchanan. He'd liked the boy, Jimmy, too. Someone had a lot to answer for and if it was the last thing he did on this earth, the bastard was going to answer for it. He glanced over his shoulder at the bodies laid out on top of the coach. Since the stage was only half full—most carried up to nine passengers inside and more outside and on the roof—all the bags and luggage were in the boot and there was plenty of room on top for the dead lawman and the dead passenger. He frowned and faced front.

Lights twinkled ahead. That would be Arklin Station.

Fargo imagined that the man who ran it was wondering why they were so late getting there.

Arklin didn't have a wife. He had a black helper, a former slave. They helped take the bodies off and put them in the stable and Arklin said he would bury them as soon as the stage left. He pestered Fargo with questions until Fargo had enough and told him to go on about his work.

Fargo was sipping his third cup of piping hot coffee when the chair across from him scraped.

"I thought you could use some company."

"You thought wrong."

Melissa blinked but sat anyway. "You're taking the deaths awful hard."

"Am I?"

"God, you're in a funk. What can I do to lighten your mood?"

"Find a cliff and jump off it."

Melissa's pretty features hardened. "Here now. That's no way to talk to a friend."

"Is that what you are?"

"Now you're being cruel. I didn't think you had it in you to treat someone this way."

Fargo swallowed and set the cup down. "You have no idea how cruel I can be."

"Well, I can be cruel, too. Instead of sitting there feeling sorry for yourself, shouldn't you be thinking about the passengers? About our safety, I mean. Three of those robbers are still alive. How do we know they won't try again before we reach Denver?"

Fargo had to admit she had a point but he would be damned if he'd tell her she did. "I'll protect you."

"Like you protected Floyd?"

The simmering cauldron deep in Fargo threatened to boil over—Floyd Weems was the dead passenger. "Are you worried about your own ass?"

"Don't be crude. I'm worried about all of us. That man in black is hell in spurs."

"His days are numbered."

"You're that sure of yourself?" Melissa shook her head. "I'm sorry, but I don't share your confidence. So far you haven't done much of anything except antagonize people. Marshal Shicklin. William Mercer, I hear. And my fellow passengers aren't too fond of you, either, at the moment."

"They can go to hell and you can, too."

Melissa pushed back her chair and stood. "Here I'm trying to help and you treat me like this."

Fargo felt a slight prick of conscience and smothered it. He finished the cup and poured another and was starting on that when Arklin came in.

"The stage is ready. Do you want me to send my helper up to Oro City to tell Miss Randall about the attack?"

"She'll find out anyway when I get back. Better keep your man here, just in case."

"In case what?"

"So far, whoever is trying to ruin the Colorado Stage Company has only attacked the stages. Sooner or later it might

110

sink in that a better way would be to burn down the relay stations."

Arklin blanched. "Say, I hadn't thought of that. If they burn us down, Miss Randall couldn't afford to rebuild." He scratched his head. "Why do you suppose they haven't tried that already?"

"I don't know," Fargo said. But a possible answer occurred to him, and if he was right, it changed how he should look at things.

"Should I load the passengers?"

"Go ahead. I'll be right out." As Arklin turned to go Fargo added, "No one rides on top. One of the women might want to but you're to tell her no."

"Yes, sir."

They got under way. The peaks were black silhouettes against the blue black of the sky. Owls hooted and coyotes yowled and now and again a wolf added to the wilderness refrain.

Fargo didn't light the candle lamps. The glow could be seen from a long way off. There was enough light from the stars and a sliver of moon to see by.

Oro City was about a hundred miles from Denver and the relay stations were spaced about equal distances apart. They reached the next toward the middle of the night. The passengers were sleepy and surly and filed in without saying much.

Fargo sat by himself and downed more coffee. He needed it more than ever.

The station was run by a Mrs. Latham. A widow, she was kindly and prim and relied on her three sons to do most of the work. She came and sat with him.

"Are you all right?"

Fargo grunted.

"I don't mean to pry but you look grumpy as can be."

Fargo told her about Buchanan and the passenger.

"This whole affair is terrible," Mrs. Latham said sadly. "People shot, lives lost, and for what?" She sighed and remarked to herself, "I've always had a suspicion that man must have something to do with it."

"What man?"

"The one who came around asking questions before all this started."

Fargo sat up. "I'd like to hear about him."

"One day the stage pulled in from Denver and a man got out. About your age, maybe a little younger. He was nattily dressed and carried a cane."

Fargo recollected that Gil Whitten carried a cane. "Go on, ma'am."

"Well, the coach was full, so I had my hands busy with feeding the passengers. But this man didn't eat. He followed me around, asking all sorts of questions. How long had I run the relay station? How many stages came through a day? How many passengers usually got off? Those sorts of things."

"What did you tell him?"

"I answered him the best I could but it got so he was underfoot and a nuisance. Finally I told him I had work to do and to quit pestering me. He went on to Oro City and it wasn't long after that the first of our stages was robbed."

"You let Brandy Randall know?"

"Why, no, I didn't. All I have is my suspicion. I don't even remember his name."

Fargo made a mental note to ask the other station managers whether they had been questioned by the same gent.

"What will come of all this, Mr. Fargo? Will Miss Randall have to close down?"

"Not if I can help it." Fargo excused himself and went out to stretch his legs. The cool air was bracing. Over by the stage, the farmer and a townsman were talking. Mrs. Latham's sons were switching the horses. He stretched and walked around to the corral and put a foot on the bottom rail and his arms on the top one.

A dress swished and Melissa was next to him. "Can we talk or will you bite my head off?"

"Your tit, maybe, but not your head."

Her mouth fell and she uttered a short laugh. "You just say whatever pops into your head, don't you?"

"You have nice tits."

Melissa laughed louder and shook her head in wonder. "Is this your idea of sweet talk? After how you treated me earlier, you have your nerve."

"Want to go for a walk in the woods?"

"Here and now? Be serious. The stage leaves soon."

"Not for ten or fifteen minutes yet," Fargo said. "And not without me."

"You're unbelievable."

Fargo bent and kissed her on the mouth. "What do you say?"

"I say no."

He kissed her again, letting the kiss linger, and rimmed her lips with his tongue. "What do you say now?"

"I say you are insane. And I want to know why. At the last station you gave me the notion you hate my guts."

Fargo caressed her hair and her neck. She shivered, but not from the cool air. "I can tell you want to."

"I'm not a hussy, thank you very much."

Running his hand over her shoulder and down her arm, Fargo clasped her hand. "We had fun last time, didn't we?" He pulled but she didn't move.

"All it is for you is sex. You don't care about me at all."

"Ten minutes," Fargo said. "A quick one." He pulled on her hand again.

"Men," Melissa said.

Fargo kissed her ear and her neck and her cheek. "It will relax you, help you sleep."

"Why don't you say it will clear up my complexion while you're at it?" she scoffed. But she also grinned.

"What do you like more than gushing?"

"Oh God."

Fargo pulled and she took a few steps and stopped. "It will make this a night you'll never forget."

Melissa laughed. "You're using every old line there is. Why don't you come right out and give me the real reason?"

"I want to fuck you."

"That's it? That's all? You don't love me or think I'm the most beautiful woman there ever was?"

"You're not."

Melissa drew back. "You can go to hell. A gal likes to be sweet-talked. She likes a meal out, and flowers, and a walk in the moonlight. Not to be treated like a bitch in heat."

"I would never treat you like that," Fargo said, and placed her hand on his iron-hard manhood.

Melissa gave a start and her strawberry lips parted in an

O of surprise. She swallowed, and glared at him, and said, "Damn you, anyhow."

"You're not pulling your hand away."

"I hate you."

"Do you hate this, too?" Fargo said, and moved her hand up and down.

"I could just shoot you."

Fargo kissed her and she kissed him back, her ardor rising the longer the kiss went on. When they broke she was panting and her hand was still on his throbbing manhood. "Ready to ride me until you come?"

Melissa smiled and leaned against him and said huskily, "Baby, give it to Momma."

20

Thick forest grew close to the corral. Fargo drew Melissa under a white fir and pressed her against the trunk and she molded her hot mouth to his in hungry need. With one hand she pried at his buckle while with the other she went on stroking him.

Fargo didn't bother with her buttons and stays. He covered her right breast and squeezed and she uttered a low moan. He cupped her bottom and she ground harder.

"Yes," Melissa breathed in his ear. "Oh, God, yes."

Their lips locked anew. Fargo hiked at her dress and her chemise, thankful she wasn't wearing a crinoline. His hand brushed bare skin and he caressed her silken inner thigh. The longer he caressed, the hotter she became.

There was a shout from the front of the station and Melissa stiffened.

"They're looking for us."

"It was something about the horses." Fargo wouldn't stop even if they were.

"We should stop."

To shut her up Fargo kissed her and slid his hand up her thigh. Gradually she relaxed. Her hands were everywhere; her lips smothered his face and his throat.

Fargo needed this. He needed to take his mind off the so-called Stagecoach War. He needed to stop thinking about Big Jim and the passenger. He got her dress up around her waist and she got his pants down around his knees. Her fingers closed on his pulsing organ and she cupped him down low.

A great roaring was in Fargo's ears. Spreading her thighs, he touched the tip to her slit and she gasped in carnal craving.

"I want it. I want all of it."

Fargo rammed in and up, impaling her. Her head fell back and her mouth parted in a silent expression of raw rapture. Her moist walls were a velvet glove. When he rocked on his heels, thrusting in and out, she dug her nails into his arms. She also sank her teeth into his shoulder, no doubt to keep from crying out.

Fargo stroked faster. Any moment, someone could come looking for them.

Melissa wrapped her legs and moved in rhythm. "Do me," she said. "Do me hard."

The night seemed to fold in on them, giving Fargo the illusion there was him and her and nothing else. The exquisite softness of her wet sheath drove him to molten heights. He rammed harder and faster and harder and faster. Her teeth bit deeper. Sliding a hand between their bodies, he rubbed her tiny knob. Suddenly she exploded. She writhed and pumped and mewed and sucked in great breaths and spurted and spurted. A minute after she crested, a keg of powder went off between his legs.

In slow motion they coasted to a stop.

Melissa leaned her forehead on his chest and lowered her legs. "Damn, that was good."

"You're not bad yourself."

Melissa grinned. "Does this mean I get to ride on top now?"

"No."

"I could just slap you." Melissa pushed him back. "I give myself to you and you don't even care."

"It's not safe on the box."

"Safe enough for you," she said as she smoothed her dress and fluffed her hair.

"Who the hell else is going to drive the stage?" Fargo put his hand on her arm. "We've already lost two people and those who killed them are still out there." He didn't mention that there might be someone behind them, as well.

"That's why you don't want me up on the seat with you? You're afraid something will happen to me?" Melissa smiled and kissed him on the mouth. "That's sweet. So you do give a damn, after all."

Fargo let her believe what she wanted. He pulled himself together and they walked around the corral to the front of the station. The other passengers were idling by the stage.

Mrs. Latham spotted him and came over. "You're all set." She glanced at Melissa. "Did you enjoy your stroll?"

"Bet your fanny I did," Melissa answered, and chuckled and walked on.

"My, what a tart young woman," Mrs. Latham said. "What does she do for a living? I wonder."

"Wriggles her backside," Fargo said.

Mrs. Latham snorted and covered her mouth with her hand. "You're not suggesting she's a—how shall I put this delicately? A lady of the night?"

"No, but she would be good at it if she was."

"What a terrible thing to say." Mrs. Latham stared after Melissa. "I have the strangest feeling I've seen her somewhere."

"She brought her grandma up from Denver less than a week ago," Fargo mentioned.

"No. Not that recent." Mrs. Latham rubbed her chin. "Months ago, it was."

"Driver!" the townsman over by the stage hollered. "Are we leaving sometime this year? I have an important appointment in Denver tomorrow."

"Get in the damn stage, then," Fargo said. He said good-bye to Mrs. Latham and regained his roost. As soon as the stage door closed he flicked the whip and the team surged into motion.

Mrs. Latham waved.

At one point on the next leg the road ran for hundreds of yards along the rim of a precipice. A misstep on the part of the horses would result in calamity.

Only when the cliff was behind them did Fargo breathe easy. Later he had switchbacks to deal with, and steep slopes where he once again had to ride the brake. And then there was a section where a rock slide covered half the road.

The fourth relay station was nestled in the foothills. This one was run by a bearded bear who barked orders at his helpers and treated the passengers as if they were an inconvenience.

Fargo filled a cup to the brim with coffee and went back

out and sat on a bench near the door. He told himself that he should nap for an hour but as tired as he was, he didn't feel like sleeping.

The manager came out and plopped on the bench beside him.

"I just heard about the two passengers you lost."

"Sykes, isn't it?" Fargo said.

The man nodded. "Knew Brandywine's pa, and it was him hired me. I run a tight station."

"Good for you."

Sykes harrumphed. "You're only filling in for the regular driver so I won't take offense at your tone."

"I don't give a good damn what you take offense at," Fargo said.

"You have no call to treat me like this."

"I didn't lose anybody. They were killed."

"You're the driver. Everything that happens on your stage, you're responsible for."

"Like hell," Fargo said. "Did I ask those robbers to try and rob it?"

"Maybe if you'd stopped those two would still be alive. By trying to outrun the robbers, you invited them to shoot at you."

"Go away."

"I was a driver once. I know what I'm talking about. It all comes down to us on the box."

"Second warning," Fargo said.

"Damn it, son. I'm not out to rile you. But Brandy's not going to like it one little bit. The law will get involved, and it will cause her all sorts of headaches."

The last thing Fargo wanted to hear was how poor a job he was doing. He debated slugging the old rooster but drank more coffee instead.

To the east the sky was brightening. Nearer, a quarter of a mile or so, was a cluster of lights and buildings.

Sykes saw him looking and said, "That's a relay for the Cobb and Whitten line. They only have three between Denver and Oro City. Cheap bastards."

"Do you pay much attention to who goes in and out of there?"

"Their stages go by all the time. And I see those two with their fancy clothes and fancy canes now and then."

"Two?" Fargo said.

"Whitten and Cobb. They're the owners. Don't you know anything?"

"They both carry canes?"

"A lot of young gents do. Me, I never saw much use for them. My legs work fine."

"Are they always together?"

"Not always, no. Sometimes it's the one and sometimes it's the other."

"You can tell them apart?"

"Cobb is a little younger. And he's got the sort of looks women swoon over."

"You don't say."

"I just did."

Fargo got up and went in. Melissa was at a table with the other passengers, talking to the dumpling in a bonnet. He sat near them and set his cup down.

"Ladies."

"To what do we owe this honor?" the dumpling asked. Her name, Fargo recollected, was Ethel. "Usually you keep to yourself."

Fargo ignored her and focused on Melissa. "How well do you know Whitten and Cobb?"

Her brow furrowed and she pursed her lips. "I've seen them around town. Why?"

"Is it true they both carry canes?"

Melissa snickered. "Canes are all the fashion these days. You know that. Gamblers, doctors, lots of men carry them."

"Do Whitten and Cobb?"

"I believe Gil and Tyree both do, yes."

"Cobb's first name is Tyree?" Fargo couldn't recall hearing it.

"Tyree Madison Cobb is his full name. He's from Indiana. His father runs a stage line there. It's where Tyree learned the business."

"You know a lot about him."

Melissa colored slightly. "That's just what I've heard. Saloon gossip, mostly. I hear a lot of it, as you should have learned by now."

"Have I ever," Fargo said.

Ethel cleared her throat. "What you just said isn't entirely true, dearie."

Fargo and Melissa both turned and said at the same time, "What?"

"I've seen you a couple of times with Mr. Cobb. You were walking down the street, and talking."

"You're mistaken," Melissa said.

"No, I'm positive it was you," Ethel insisted. "And I know Mr. Cobb on sight. He's so handsome. A person doesn't forget a dashing figure of a man like him."

Melissa's mouth became a slit. "You're mistaken, I tell you."

"And I tell you I'm not."

Suddenly smacking the table, Melissa got up and bustled out.

"What in the world was that all about?" Ethel asked, shocked.

Fargo wished to hell he knew.

"Here we were getting along so nicely, too. Some people sure are strange, aren't they?"

"Lady," Fargo said. "You have no idea."

21

Fargo had never been so happy to see Denver. From a distance it sprawled like the squares of a random checkerboard. Some of the buildings were two and three stories high.

The newspapers were crowing about how the city was growing by leaps and bounds. The recent gold rush had a lot to do with it. The population was now over three thousand, with predictions that it would continue to swell. Within another decade, it was claimed, it would be the leading city between the Mississippi River and the Pacific Ocean.

Denver was famous for being wild and unruly. It was no secret that the criminal element had its fingers in just about everything. Vices were encouraged. Saloons, gambling houses, and brothels outnumbered churches and schools by twenty to one. There were so many brothels that the city was known far and wide as the biggest whorehouse anywhere.

As far as the government went, it was part of the Territory of Kansas. It had a marshal and he had deputies but they were few and the criminals were many. The lawmen did their best but it was like trying to stop an avalanche with a feather.

The Colorado Stage Company office was at the northeast end of Larimer Street. To get there Fargo had to take the bridge across Cherry Creek. The man who ran it, Brandy had told him, was Hiram Parks. Parks was stout and all business. As soon as the stage came to a stop, Parks had men tending to the passengers and the team.

Fargo wearily climbed down. He was to take the run up to Oro City the next day and he needed sleep. At the back of the station was a small room with cots for the drivers, and he sought one out. The moment he closed his eyes he was asleep.

A sound woke him.

The room was dark. Fargo lay there groggy and stiff and tried to get his brain to work. Rising on his elbows, he glanced at the small window. Twilight had fallen. He'd slept most of the day away.

Rising, Fargo yawned and shuffled into the office. Parks was at his desk, writing, and looked up and nodded.

On a small stove in the corner was a pot of coffee. Fargo helped himself and straddled a chair. "I feel like death warmed over."

"You look it, too," Parks said. "Are you sure you'll be up to taking the stage tomorrow?"

Fargo stared at him.

"Just asking. Most folks don't realize how hard it is, being a driver. They think all a man has to do is sit up there and use the whip now and again. But there's a hell of a lot more to it."

"Amen to that," Fargo said as the hot coffee seared him in welcome relief.

"I know you don't drive stages for a living but you did good, mister. You even brought the stage in on time. Rafer, himself, doesn't always do that."

"I had to push to make up the time we lost," Fargo mentioned.

"Then you did double good. That road ain't for amateurs. You could make a living at this if you wanted."

"No, thanks," Fargo said. "I'd rather have a horse under me than a stage."

Parks put down his pencil. "Let's talk about something else. I reported the killings to the marshal and the sheriff. The marshal can't do much since it was outside his jurisdiction. Sheriff Wynkoop says he'll have a deputy look into it but not to get our hopes up unless you can identify the robbers."

"They were wearing bandannas."

"Then whoever they were, they'll likely get away with it. Which is a damn shame."

"No," Fargo said. "They won't."

"How will you find them?"

"There are ways," Fargo said, and let it go at that. He finished his coffee and refilled his cup and went out. A street lamp was being lit and lights were coming on all over. He stood and gulped and felt his blood begin to flow.

Parks came outside. "I can recommend a place to eat if you want."

"Food can wait," Fargo said. "I want to know about a saloon."

"Just one? Hell, there must be thirty or more."

"Which one is the worst?"

"Worst how? The one that only serves watered-down whiskey? The one that has the ugliest doves? What?"

"The saloon where the killers and footpads and confidence men go to drink," Fargo clarified. Nearly every big city had watering holes where the criminal element, as the newspapers called them, socialized. Places where no honest citizen would set foot.

"Several have bad reputations."

"Which has the worst?"

"The Inferno on Arapaho Street," Parks said without hesitation. "The marshal won't set foot in it. There are knifings and shootings all the time. Anyone goes in there, they take their life in their hands."

Fargo drained the cup and handed it to Parks. "If I'm not back by daylight, find another driver."

"Hold on," Parks said, taking hold of his arm. "What are you thinking of doing?"

Fargo stared at Parks' hand and he removed it.

"You cause trouble in the Inferno and blood will be spilled."

"I'm counting on it," Fargo said, "since I plan to do some of the spilling."

Denver's night life was astir. Two-legged predators were coming out of their rooms and apartments to prowl the city's byways. Women in tight dresses paraded their wares. Voices and occasional bursts of music filled the air.

Fargo turned left at the first intersection. Two blocks brought him to Arapaho. It was wilder and noisier and the ladies of the night were more brazen. A pair came up to him, smiling and asking if there was anything they could do for him, and when he declined, a pert blonde rubbed herself against him and promised to take him around the world and back. He smiled and swatted her fanny and said maybe another time.

The Inferno lived up to its name. Never in all his travels had Fargo come across a saloon painted entirely in red. Walls, false front, the batwings, everything was red. Hard-faced men lounged in the shadows.

Fargo pushed on the batwings and took a step and stopped. "I'll be damned." The inside was as red as the outside: walls, ceilings, bar, tables, even the chairs. The doves wore red dresses and the bartenders wore red jackets.

A brunette with dilated eyes swished her hips up to him and crooked her finger under his chin. "See anything you like, big man?"

"I have died and gone to hell," Fargo said.

She laughed much too loud. "How about buying a girl a drink?"

"Why not?"

The bar was crowded. Fargo took her around to the far end where he could see the entire room. A man with cold eyes was already there.

"Shoo," Fargo said.

The man looked at him. "What did you say?"

"You're standing in my spot."

"Like hell I am."

The brunette plucked at Fargo's sleeve. "We can find another. This here is Layton. You don't want to rile him."

"Darcy is right," Layton said, glowering. "You don't want to make me mad."

"If I ask you real polite, you're not going to move?" Fargo said.

Layton straightened and slid his hand under his jacket. "Get out of here, jackass, before I bury you."

Fargo drew his Colt and slammed the barrel against Layton's head. Layton collapsed without a sound. Reaching down, Fargo dragged him over against the wall and left him lying there. He returned to the end of the bar, twirled the Colt into his holster, and faced Layton's astonished friends. "Any of you want to join him?"

They looked at one another and left.

Laughing merrily, Darcy wrapped her arm around his. "Damn, that was slick. But when Layton comes around he'll likely want to kill you."

"Other one," Fargo said.

"I beg your pardon."

"Hold my other arm. Not my gun arm."

Darcy gave a start. "Oh. Sorry. Most men don't care one way or the other." She moved from his right side to his left and hooked her elbow with his. "How about that drink?"

Fargo paid for a bottle and filled her glass and then his. He took a slow sip while taking the measure of the Inferno's customers. Parks had been right. This was the worst saloon in the city. It was a den of human wolves.

There was a city ordinance against carrying weapons but Fargo didn't doubt for a second that nearly every man there was heeled with either a revolver or a blade. Some were easy to spot; their coats and shirts and pants bulged where they shouldn't.

Darcy downed her glass and held it out for a refill. "What would you like to talk about, handsome?"

"Black dusters."

She cocked her head. "Are you looking to buy one? Because they don't sell dusters in saloons." She cackled loudly at her joke.

"Seen anyone wearing a black duster tonight?"

"Can't say as I have, no." She grinned and patted his sleeve. "You looking for a friend of yours or something?"

"Or something," Fargo said.

A tall man in a frock coat and string tie was coming down the bar. His coat didn't bulge but the butt of a revolver poked from under it.

"Uh-oh," Darcy said, and drew back. "It's the owner. Mr. Oliver."

The tall man stopped and stared at Layton and then at Fargo. He had cold eyes and a scar above an eyebrow. "Evening, friend."

"Nice place you have," Fargo said. "But it could do with more red."

Oliver looked him up and down. "I saw what you did. You're mighty quick with that pistol of yours."

"Clean living."

Oliver wasn't amused. "I don't like trouble. Cause any more and you'll answer to me and my helpers." He pointed at several men in red jackets.

"Might be you and them aren't enough," Fargo said.

"I have more."

"Call them."

"I'm not sure I like you, friend," Oliver said resentfully. "Finish your drink and get out."

Fargo set his glass on the bar and lowered his hand so it brushed his holster. "Start the dance."

Oliver's eyes darted to the Colt. "You're that sure of yourself?"

"I have reason to be."

"I don't much like braggarts," Oliver said. "How about you prove it to me?"

"Anytime."

"How about now?" Oliver said, and his hand rose to his revolver.

22

The click of Fargo's Colt hammer was loud enough that those near the bar looked around in alarm. "You don't want to do that."

Oliver had turned to stone. "Christ Almighty," he said breathlessly. "No one is that fast."

Fargo did a forward twirl and a reverse twirl and a spin that ended with the Colt back in his holster. "Want to see it again?"

"No," Oliver said, and licked his lips. "Who the hell are you?"

"All you need to know," Fargo said, "is that the next son of a bitch who draws on me will get a lead pill for what ails him."

"Ails him?" Darcy asked, earning a sharp glance from her employer.

"A case of stupid."

Darcy tittered. "That's a good one. I ain't ever heard it before." She rubbed his left arm. "I sure am taking a shine to you. You don't bore me like most men do."

"Stick around," Fargo said. "It might get even more interesting."

Oliver cleared his throat. "I have work to do," he said, and turned to go.

"Hold on," Fargo said. "I'm looking for a man in a black duster. Have you seen him?"

"Mister, look around you. There must be sixty, seventy people. They come and they go and I don't pay much attention except when they act up." Oliver smoothed his frock coat and adjusted his tie and mingled.

"Never thought I'd see the day," Darcy said.

"Wednesday?"

"No, silly goose. The day that Ira Oliver was scared. He's scared of you, though. I could tell."

Fargo refilled their glasses and raised his. "How about a toast?"

Darcy raised hers. "To what? A night in bed together? I'm all for that."

"To men who are as slow as molasses and to women who are as fast as sin."

Darcy giggled. "Oh. I get it." She did more cackling and almost spilled her drink.

Fargo reckoned he would be there a while. He'd rather have a table but all the tables were full. "Bring the bottle," he said, and drifted over to where five men were playing poker.

He watched a while and when one of them went all in and lost, he claimed the man's seat.

Darcy moved behind his chair and began massaging the back of his neck.

Fargo didn't show his poke. Not in a place like the Inferno. He kept it in his pocket and fished inside for a few bills. Over the next hour and a half he won some hands and he lost some.

Oliver and an underling in red hovered for a while and drifted off.

Then Fargo was dealt three fours, a jack, and a queen. He asked for two cards and the dealer slid them across: a pair of tens. Fargo met each call but he didn't raise until the pot had grown to over two hundred dollars. He pushed in another hundred and fifty.

The other players folded save one. He fancied himself a cardsharp and had bragged about how good he was. "I'll see your raise and raise you another thirty."

Fargo was confident in his full house. Plus he had a hunch the man was bluffing. He added the thirty and they flipped their cards over.

The other player had two pair.

Darcy squealed in delight as Fargo raked in his winnings. "This is your lucky night."

Not to Fargo's way of thinking. He'd kept an eye on the batwings the whole time and no one wearing a black duster entered or left. Maybe he was wrong, he told himself. Maybe the man in black wasn't the hard case he took him to be.

Fargo got up and roved. He played roulette. He bucked the tiger.

Darcy stayed glued to him as if afraid he would run off.

By midnight the Inferno was wall to wall. A cloud of cigar smoke hung over the tables. The piano player was tired and missed a few notes and the doves were starting to drag.

Not Darcy. She clung to him, as perky as ever, and now and again pressed her lips to his neck.

A corner table opened. Fargo hurried over before someone else claimed it. A man in a bowler was about to when Fargo slipped past him and sat down first.

"That's a low trick," the man objected. "I wanted this table for myself."

"There are still three empty chairs," Fargo said. "Pick one."

The man hesitated and then glanced at Darcy and grinned. "Thaddeus Brown. I live here in Denver. Work in dry goods."

"And you come to a saloon like this one?" Fargo said.

Brown fumbled in his jacket, looked around to be sure no one was watching, and showed Fargo a derringer. "I carry protection."

"For flies," Fargo said.

"The man who sold it to me said I could drop a bear with it."

"If the bear was the size of your thumb."

Brown shoved the derringer back in his pocket. "I'm quite happy with it."

"Have you ever shot it?"

"Why would I want to do that?"

Darcy waggled her glass for more whiskey and Fargo poured.

"Say, handsome. What color did you say that duster was you're interested in?"

"Black."

"What kind of hat does the man have?"

"Black, too. Black shirt. Black pants. Black boots."

Fargo offered the whiskey to Brown and he shook his head.

"Well, I'll be," Darcy said. "First Layton and then the cards and now this."

"Are you talking nonsense or is it something I am supposed to understand?"

"I'm trying to tell you that a man wearing a black duster and a black hat with a wide brim just came in."

Fargo shot to his feet. It was true. A man in black and two others were making their way to the bar. He couldn't see their faces. "Stay here," he said, and moved to cut them off. There were too many people.

Fargo changed direction and reached the near end of the bar about the same time they reached the middle. He planted himself and put his hand on his Colt. About a dozen drinkers were between him and them. He tapped the one next to him on the shoulder.

The man glanced around. "What the hell do you want?"

"Move. And pass it on."

"What?"

"I want you to move," Fargo said. "Pass it on to the man next to you and have him pass it down the bar."

"Why should I—" The man looked at Fargo's hand on the Colt and at Fargo's face and his Adam's apple bobbed and he said, "Whatever you say." He turned and spoke to the next man and quickly backed away. The next man did the same thing; he looked at Fargo and at the Colt and he passed it on to the next. In a surprisingly short time that end of the bar was empty.

Fargo moved closer. The man in black had his back to him and didn't notice but one of the others did. The man reacted as if he had been punched and said something to the one in black.

The man in black turned.

By then whispers had spread and most everyone had caught on that trouble was brewing.

In the quiet that fell, Fargo's voice cracked like a whip. "Jack Santor."

Santor didn't act at all surprised. He smirked and hooked his thumb in his gun belt inches from his ivory-handled Smith & Wesson. "Look who it is."

"Nice duster," Fargo said. "Do you wear it to bed, too?"

Santor's eyes were spikes of spite. "You'd be smart to make yourself scarce."

"No," Fargo said. "The smart thing is to bury you."

Oliver and a pair of men in red jackets pushed through the onlookers and Oliver moved between Fargo and Santor. "What's going on here?" He glared at Fargo. "I told you I don't want trouble."

"You see that gent in the duster?"

Oliver turned toward Santor. "What about him?"

"He likes to rob stages and shoot people. He killed two who were on the last stage from Oro City."

"That true, mister?"

"Hell, no," Santor said. "Whoever that hombre is, he must be whiskey soaked."

"He says he didn't do it," Oliver said to Fargo.

"Get out of the way."

"Now you hold on. Whatever is going on between you two, take it outside."

Jack Santor motioned at his companions and they spread out, their gun hands at their sides.

"I won't have gunplay in here," Oliver said. "Whenever there's a shooting the city council makes a fuss about closing me down."

"Move," Fargo said.

"Damn it." Oliver drew himself up to his full height. "I want all four of you out of my saloon."

"You stay there, you'll take a slug," Fargo warned him.

Oliver turned to Santor again. "Will *you* at least listen to reason? Take your friends and go."

"And disappoint this bastard?" Santor said, nodding at Fargo.

Oliver turned to a man in a red jacket. "Mr. Collins, get them the hell out of here."

"Yes, sir." Collins started to reach under his red jacket. Just like that, the ivory-handled Colt was in Santor's hand. It boomed and Collins' shoulder belched blood and he staggered against Oliver and both of them fell against the bar.

In a twinkling Fargo had his Colt up and out. But he didn't have a clear shot at Santor. Oliver and the other man were in the way. One of Santor's friends fired and the lead buzzed his ear. He replied in kind, the Colt bucking twice, and at the second shot the center of the man's forehead dissolved.

Santor and the other man were shooting but not at Fargo. Santor shot Oliver and Oliver screamed and fell.

Fargo backpedaled. This wasn't what he'd wanted. It was supposed to be him and the stage robbers and no one else. He ducked around the end of the bar as a slug bit into the wood.

A woman shrieked and there was a mass exodus for the batwings.

Fargo rose high enough to see over the top. Santor and his friend were retreating toward the far end and firing at Oliver's men. Oliver had a hand to his throat, blood spurting in a torrent.

Fargo aimed and fired and Santor's companion clutched his chest and dropped. He aimed at Santor but the man in black had more lives than a cat and darted through a doorway.

Fargo gave chase. Before he had taken three strides another red jacket blocked his way.

"Stop right there!" the man cried, and pointed a six-shooter.

23

Fargo shot him in the shoulder. The man cried out and staggered and Fargo shoved him aside and ran on. He gambled that Santor wasn't waiting to shoot him on the other side of the door and he hurtled on through. At the far end of a long hall another door was closing.

Fargo's leg was hurting but it bore his weight well. At the door he stepped to one side and flung it wide. When no shots boomed he stuck his head past the jamb.

A dark side street ran in both directions. Maybe a dozen people were about. None of them was running.

Fargo crouched and went out low and fast. Down the street to his right a pistol cracked and a slug smacked the wall. He didn't answer it but he did fly toward the gun flash, zigzagging as he went. Some shouts broke the night, the strollers wanting to know who was shooting and why.

Fargo came to a fence. He took another gamble and flew past it but no one was there. He stopped and hunkered and looked and listened but Jack Santor was gone.

Fargo swore. It had all been for nothing. He reloaded and rose and returned to the stage station by way of side streets and alleys.

Parks wasn't there. Apparently he had gone home for the night.

Fargo poured coffee and sat in a chair, pondering. He was getting nowhere. Santor was still out there and would undoubtedly try to hold up another stage as part of the plan to shut down the Colorado Stage Company. But whose plan? William Mercer's, the banker who had financed Cobb and Whitten? Or was Santor working for Cobb and Whitten?

Then there was the half-breed, Tangwaci. Who was he working for? And why had the breed tried to kill him? As if all that wasn't enough of a headache, Miles Blackburn and Hitch wanted his hide, too, and he had no idea why.

Fargo shook his head and did more swearing. It was too damn complicated. Or was it? Maybe there was something he was missing, something that would make sense of the whole mess. But for the life of him, he couldn't figure out what.

Fargo sighed and finished his coffee and went to the back room to catch some sleep. The room was dark and he didn't bother to light the lamp. The light spilling from the office was enough for him to see the cot. He was almost to it when a floorboard to his left creaked and he turned just as a blocky shadow sprang with a knife glittering dully in one hand.

It was Tangwaci.

Fargo got his hand up and grabbed the breed's wrist and Tangwaci grabbed his. Locked together, they grappled.

Tangwaci grinned savagely and hissed through clenched teeth. "Now you die, white dog."

Fargo hooked his foot behind the breed's leg but Tangwaci executed an agile hop and didn't go down. They crashed against a cot. They crashed against another. Their struggling and spinning brought them to the doorway and through it into the office.

Fargo rammed a knee at Tangwaci's groin but Tangwaci shifted and took the brunt on his leg. Growling like a rabid wolf, Tangwaci drove his knee at Fargo's groin. Fargo twisted but he wasn't quite quick enough. Pain burst like a cannon shell. Through sheer force of will he stayed on his feet. They smashed against the desk. They sent a chair toppling. They wrenched this way and that and suddenly they were next to the stove.

Fargo glanced at the coffeepot. It was still half full.

Bunching his shoulders, he shoved, hurling Tangwaci back.

Before the breed could recover, Fargo grabbed the coffeepot by the handle and threw the hot coffee into his face.

Tangwaci howled. He frantically wiped at his eyes with his sleeve and blindly groped about.

Fargo kicked him in the knee. Tangwaci screeched and

buckled, his head an inviting target. Fargo swept his Colt up and around and brought it crashing down with the force of a sledge hammer.

Fargo's leg was hurting again and he was breathing heavily. He stared grimly down at the unconscious form and said, "I've got you now, you son of a bitch."

A rope hung on a peg. Fargo took it down and cut off two pieces, one piece to tie the breed's wrists behind his back and the other to tie his legs. Stepping back, he picked up the coffeepot and put fresh coffee on to brew.

Ten minutes later Fargo was sitting and drinking when Tangwaci Smith twitched and stirred and groaned. Tangwaci opened his eyes, realized he was bound, and frenziedly tugged at the ropes. His eyes were pools of hate.

"White bastard."

"Who hired you?" Fargo asked.

"Go to hell."

"I saw you at Brandy's. You tried to kill me at the stage stable, and now this." Fargo sipped and remembered the flashes of light on the mountain. "You followed me down from Oro City, didn't you? You were behind the stage the whole time?"

Tangwaci jutted his chin defiantly and didn't say a word.

"You're going to tell me," Fargo said.

"I not talk," Tangwaci said smugly. "You give me to tin star I not say to him."

"Who said anything about handing you over to the marshal or the sheriff?"

A hint of confusion came into Tangwaci's dark eyes. "What you do, then?"

"We're going to talk, you and me."

"You big fool."

"We'll see about that." Fargo set the cup on the table. Bending, he pulled his pant leg up and drew the Arkansas toothpick from the ankle sheath.

"What you do?"

Fargo held the toothpick so the blade gleamed in the light.

"I lived with an Apache band for a spell once. I've lived with the Sioux, too." He paused. "Ever seen what they do to their enemies?"

"You try scare Tangwaci," Tangwaci said. "But you white. You not Apache. You not Lakota. You not do same they do."

Fargo rose and hunkered next to him. "You'd like to think that, wouldn't you? But you're proof that you're wrong."

"How me proof?" Tangwaci asked uncertainly.

"You've lived with whites. You wear white clothes, you act like a white at times. The same with me. I've lived with Apaches. I can act like an Apache when I want to."

"White not Apache. Silly talk. I not afraid."

"How about now?" Fargo said, and sank the blade to the hilt in the breed's leg and held it there.

Tangwaci arched his back and his mouth parted in a silent scream.

Fargo twisted and Tangwaci hissed and thrashed and glared. "Are you afraid yet?"

Tangwaci was red in the face and spittle dribbled down his chin. He said something in Ute and then switched to English. "I kill you. I kill you dead."

"You're welcome to try." Fargo pulled the knife out. A lot of blood came with it but not enough to be life-threatening.

He wiped the blade on Tangwaci's shirt. "Now, then. Where were we? Oh, yes. Who sent you?"

"You never know."

"Yes," Fargo said. "I will." He stabbed the breed in the other leg.

This time Tangwaci couldn't hold it in. He howled and bucked and called Fargo every cuss word and then some. When he was spent he subsided and lay with his cheek in a scarlet pool spreading under him.

"Who sent you?"

Tangwaci moved his head so his face wasn't in the blood.

"Was it William Mercer?"

"Who?" The puzzlement in Tangwaci's voice seemed genuine.

"You damn well already know," Fargo bluffed. "Mercer is one of the richest men in Oro City. He has his fingers in everything."

"Not know him."

"Then did Cobb and Whitten hire you?"

"Not know them, too."

Fargo almost stabbed him a third time. Standing, he placed his boot on the wound in Tangwaci's right leg. "I'll count to three."

"Count to hundred. It be same."

"One," Fargo said.

"You not make me say what I not want to say."

"Two."

Tangwaci spat at him. "You yellow. Cut me free. We fight man to man."

"Three," Fargo said, and put all his weight on the leg.

The breed swore and snarled and whipped about and in a couple of minutes he once again lay exhausted and caked with sweat.

"I can do this all night."

"Bastard."

"Give me the name of the man who hired you."

Tangwaci's eyes were half closed and he was breathing noisily. "Not man," he said breathlessly. "It wo—" He caught himself and stopped.

"A woman?" Fargo said. "Is that what you were about to say?"

"No."

Fargo gripped the front of the breed's shirt and sat him up with his back to a wall. "I want the truth. There's only one woman involved in this mess and that's Brandy Randall. Was it her?" He didn't see how it could be. Brandy wouldn't beg him to help her save her stage line and then try to have him killed.

"Not Brandy woman," Tangwaci said.

"I want a name."

"I want you dead."

"Was it the same person who hired Miles Blackburn and Hitch?"

"Dead, dead, dead."

Fargo caught a split second of hesitation before the man answered. "You know who they are, don't you?"

Tangwaci closed his eyes and grimaced. "Feel weak," he said. "Feel dizzy."

Fargo stepped back. There *was* an awful lot of blood.

"I'll get a sawbones if you tell me who it was."

"Eat dog shit."

"Keep wasting my time and you'll keep losing blood," Fargo warned.

The breed's eyelids fluttered. He started to keel to one side but straightened and opened his eyes. "Feel sick," he said, and retched.

"Hell," Fargo said. The stink was abominable. He opened the front door to let in air and when he turned around, Tangwaci was lying unconscious in the vomit.

"Damn it." Fargo went out into the street. Halfway up the block were several young men and he stopped them and asked if one of them would fetch a doctor.

"Are you sick, mister?"

"A man's been stabbed," Fargo explained. "He needs mending quick. I'd go myself but I don't know where any of the docs in Denver live."

"There's one not far from here," one of them said, and dashed away.

Fargo returned to the stage office and the other two followed. He took a few steps inside and drew up short in consternation.

Tangwaci wouldn't need a doctor, after all.

Someone had slit his throat from ear to ear.

24

The stage for Oro City left late.

Fargo was supposed to leave at ten in the morning but it was pushing three when he left the marshal's and three thirty when he climbed onto the box and cracked the whip.

The marshal had questioned him until Fargo was fit to throw a fit. Who had murdered Tangwaci Smith? Fargo didn't know. A man who fit Fargo's description was involved in a shooting affray at the Inferno that left four men dead and three others wounded. What did Fargo know about that? Not a thing. On and on it went until finally Fargo stood up and announced, "I have a stage to get ready. Either arrest me or let me go."

The marshal didn't like it but he walked Fargo out and at the door he said, "I happen to know Brandy Randall and I like her or I'd throw you behind bars. I wasn't born yesterday. You had something to do with that shoot-out at the saloon and now we have a dead man on our hands that you can't account for."

There were times to keep quiet and Fargo decided this was one of them.

"Get the hell out of here," the marshal said. "But I'll be checking into this and if I find you've broken the law, I'll be after you."

Fargo hadn't paid much attention to the passengers. Parks saw to getting them on the stage. It wasn't until they reached the first relay station and they filed out of the coach that he discovered there were nine—and Melissa Hart was one of them. She waited for him by the front wheel and when he alighted she clasped his hand in excitement.

"I got my dress."

"Good for you." Fargo could have done without having her on the stage. As surely as he was standing there, he knew what she would want to do.

"You sound mad at me," Melissa said. "What did I do?"

"Nothing."

"Then why treat me like I'm buffalo droppings? Two nights ago you couldn't keep your hands off me."

"A lot happened in Denver," Fargo said. He almost added that none of it was good.

"And men claim women are fickle. One day you're nice, the next you're a grump." She guided him toward the station. "Let's have a bite to eat and I'll try to ease your cares and woes."

"Why so nice?" Fargo asked.

"Does a girl need a reason?" Melissa squeezed his arm. "But if you must know, I'm glad I don't need to make any more trips to Denver. Believe it or not, I don't like taking long stage rides."

Fargo tolerated her chatter while he ate a bowl of stew. He was mopping drops of broth with a piece of bread smothered in butter when she asked the question.

"How about letting me ride up top with you?"

"No."

Melissa sat back and crossed her arms. "Here you go again. Why the hell can't I?"

"Someone is out to blow out my wick."

"That Santor character you told me about?"

"Anyone up on the box is liable to take a slug meant for me."

"What if I'm willing to take the risk?"

"I'm not." Fargo pushed the empty bowl back. "And I don't want you pestering me at every stop from here to Oro City."

"No one would shoot a woman."

Fargo stood. "We're leaving in five minutes," he announced to the rest.

"Please, Skye," Melissa said. "I'll only ask this one last time. I really don't care to ride in the stuffy old coach."

"If you need air stick your head out the window."

"I am commencing not to like you as much."

"At least you're breathing."

The next leg was downright peaceful. The grades weren't as many nor as steep as they would be higher up.

Night spread a mantle of stars over the rugged fastness of the Rockies and brought with it the usual cacophony of meat-eaters and prey.

Jack Santor didn't try to stop them. Not on that leg or the next or the last.

Shortly after noon the stage rolled down into Oro City. Once again Fargo had gone without sleep for more than twenty hours and he was bone tired.

Brandy, Rafer, and the man on crutches were waiting at the office. They tended to the team and passengers while Fargo tossed down the mail and hopped off. He had taken only a couple of steps when a dapper figure with a cane came around the stage.

"What are you doing here?" Brandy demanded.

"I need to talk to him," Gil Whitten said, nodding at Fargo.

"After I've had some sleep." Fargo went into the stable to check on the Ovaro. He spread out his bedroll and was about to lie down when Whitten came down the aisle.

"I'm sorry. It can't wait. It's all over town about Big Jim Buchanan. I liked him. I felt safe with him around. With him dead, it's only a matter of time before I'm planted, too."

"Go see your friend William Mercer," Fargo said. "Ask him why his gun hand killed Big Jim."

"That's insane," Whitten said. "Mercer put up most of the capital for our stage line. What possible reason would he have for wanting Cobb and me dead?"

"I'll find out when I pay him a visit tomorrow."

"Hold on," Whitten said. "Before you go off half-cocked, I have a proposition for you."

Fargo placed his saddle at the head of the blanket. "Make it quick."

"I'd like to hire you to take Big Jim's place."

Fargo looked at him.

"I mean it. I'll pay you two hundred a month, the same as I was paying Big Jim. All I ask is that you keep me alive until I've sorted this out."

"Why me?"

"Buchanan told me about you. You make your living as a scout but you're something of a gun hand yourself, and you've got bark on you six inches thick. What do you say? Give Brandy notice and start to work for me in the morning."

Fargo sat on the blankets and leaned back against the saddle. "No."

Whitten came closer, tapping his cane. "Damn it, man, my life is at stake. With Big Jim dead, whoever is behind this will try again, and soon."

"They might go after Brandy, too. I gave her my word I'd help her and I won't quit on her to save your bacon."

"What else am I supposed to do?" Whitten angrily demanded.

"Hire five or six toughs," Fargo said. "Shut yourself in your house or your office and don't come out until this is over."

"And when will that be? It could go on for months."

"No," Fargo said. "It won't."

"You have a crystal ball, do you, that you can predict the future?"

"I have something better. Piss."

Whitten's brow puckered. "Did you just say you have to take a leak? The outhouse is out back."

"*I'm* pissed," Fargo said. "I'm not holding back anymore. Starting tonight, I'm going to get answers."

"How?"

Fargo settled back and closed his eyes and pulled his hat brim low. "I'll come see you later on." He figured to sleep seven or eight hours and be up and about by nightfall.

"I may not be alive," Whitten said gloomily. His footsteps faded from the stable.

Sleep washed over Fargo. Occasionally a loud sound roused him but he drifted right off again.

The stalls were plunged in the gloom of twilight when he opened his eyes and sat up. He went out to the horse trough, stripped to the waist, and washed. As he was slipping his buckskin shirt back on Rafer came over.

"Have a good rest?"

"Good enough." Fargo strapped on his gun belt and jammed his hat on.

"Brandy asked me to tell you that she'd like to see you." Rafer gestured. "She's in the office."

"Anything happen while I was away?"

"It's been quiet. But I have the feelin' it won't stay that way."

Fargo went into the stable, took the Ovaro from the stall, and threw on the saddle blanket. He bent to lift the saddle.

"What are you doin'?" Rafer asked. "Didn't you hear me about Brandy?"

"Tell her I'll be right there."

"You're not runnin' out on us, are you?"

Fargo glared.

"Sorry." Rafer sheepishly nodded and turned. "I know better. Forget I said that."

Piano music wafted down the street as Fargo led the stallion from the stable to the hitch rail and looped the reins.

The door was open. Brandy was at her desk. She looked pale and drawn and had bags under her eyes. At the jingle of his spurs she stopped writing.

Fargo sat on the edge of the desk. "You should get some rest."

"When this is over or I'm dead." Brandy tiredly rubbed her face and nodded. "I'd like to hear what happened on the Denver run."

"Is that all?" Fargo got up. "It will have to wait. I have people to see."

"Who?"

"I'm starting with William Mercer and working my way from there."

"You better be careful. Marshal Shicklin is looking for an excuse to throw you behind bars."

Fargo stepped to the doorway. "One way or the other this ends by morning."

Brandy got up and came around. "I admire a man with confidence but that would take a miracle."

Fargo patted his Colt. "I've got your miracle right here."

"I was afraid of that." Brandy touched his arm. "Please don't be rash. I've grown a little fond of you."

"Just a little?" Fargo grinned and walked out.

Oro City's nightlife was astir. Painted ladies were on the prowl. So were footpads and gamblers and a host of drinkers. Yet for all the bustle it was unusually quiet.

There was little laughter and no singing. It was almost as if the city sensed that something was about to happen and was holding its collective breath.

143

Fargo chuckled at the notion. His imagination was getting the better of him. He turned left at an intersection and right at another. Houses replaced businesses. A dog barked at him from behind a porch.

Every window in William Mercer's log mansion was lit.

Fargo knocked. He didn't have long to wait before the butler opened the door.

The man didn't hide his surprise. "You again, sir?"

"Mercer here?"

"I'm sorry, but I'm afraid he gave orders that you're not to be admitted."

"Did he, now?" Fargo brushed on by into the hall.

"I'd stop right there if I were you, sir," the butler urged.

"You fixing to throw me out?"

"No, sir. But if you don't go there will be trouble."

"You have no idea," Fargo said.

25

William Mercer was in a high-backed chair with a drink in his hand and was in the act of raising the glass when Fargo walked in. "What the hell are you doing here?"

"I tried to stop him, sir," the butler said. "He refused to heed me."

"That's all right, Samuel," Mercer said. "Mr. Turner and Mr. Willow are in the kitchen. Would you fetch them for me?"

"Certainly, sir."

Mercer calmly tipped the glass and rested it on the arm of his chair. "To what do I owe your unwanted presence in my home?"

"I've got you," Fargo said.

"Do you, now?"

Fargo nodded. "Act innocent. But Santor and four others hit the stage. Since he works for you, you're the one I'm after."

"Is there a brain under that hat?"

"Where is he?" Fargo demanded.

"Where he's been since your first visit," Mercer said. "Right here, performing his duties."

"You lying son of a bitch."

William Mercer swirled the liquor in his glass and polished it off with a gulp. "I don't know what your game is. Evidently you suspect that I am behind the stage robberies, which is utterly preposterous."

"Mercer, I saw Santor in Denver with my own eyes," Fargo said. "He couldn't have been here the whole time."

"I tell you he was," the banker insisted. "If he'd gone away for several days, don't you think I would know?"

"He was in this house yesterday and the day before? You saw him? You spoke to him?"

145

Mercer hesitated. "Well, no."

"What the hell does that mean?"

"I hired eight men to protect me after the attempt on my life. They take turns, two at a time, guarding me. Santor's last turn was several days ago."

"So he could have gone to Denver and back without you knowing?"

"It is highly unlikely."

Fargo swore.

Boots scraped the wooden floor and two men wearing six-shooters came into the parlor.

"The butler said you wanted us," one of them said.

"Is this hombre giving you trouble?" asked the other.

Fargo turned to them. "Where's Jack Santor?"

"What the hell is it to you?"

Mercer got up from his chair. "I don't want this man in my home, Mr. Turner. Would you and Mr. Willow be so kind as to show him the door?"

"You heard the man," Turner said.

Fargo had no desire to shoot them but he wasn't going anywhere. "Tell us one thing first. Has Santor been here all week?"

"No, he left for a few days," Turner said.

"What's that?" William Mercer came over. "Why wasn't I told?"

Turner shrugged. "It wasn't anything worth bothering you about. He wanted some days off to visit sick kin, is all."

"They've been sick a while," the other gun hand said. "He's taken other days off, too. The rest of us cover for him."

Mercer looked sick. "What does this mean?"

Just then into the parlor came Jack Santor and two others.

Santor had on his black duster and black hat. "It means," he said scornfully, "that I can quit skulking around and do what I was hired to do."

"Mr. Santor?" Mercer said.

"Jack?" Turner echoed. "Who are these hombres with you?"

Santor sneered at Fargo. "It would have been better if I'd shot you on the stage or gunned you in Denver. But that's all right. Here or there, it's all the same."

"What is this all about?" Mercer said. "What have you been up to?"

"A smart bastard like you should have figured it out by now," Santor said. "With you and the other two out of the way, the person who hired me figures to take over the Cobb and Whitten stage line and the Colorado Stage Company, both."

"To what end?"

"What else?" Santor answered, and laughed. "Money. Each line pulls in over a thousand dollars a day on good days. That adds up."

"I can't believe this," Mercer said.

"What the hell is going on, boss?" Turner asked.

"Mr. Santor, here, has apparently been robbing stages and killing people." Mercer took a step back. "I just realized. He must be behind the attempts on my own life. To think! A viper in our midst and I never suspected."

"You talk too damn much," Santor said, and in a lightning draw he palmed his ivory-handled Smith & Wesson and shot William Mercer in the head. Quick as thought he put slugs into Turner and Willow. Willow went down but Turner stayed on his feet and tried to pull his six-shooter. The two men with Santor made sure he didn't by shooting him in the chest.

For a few seconds everyone forgot about Fargo. He took two long running bounds and dived behind the settee, unlimbering his Colt as he cleared it. Lead ripped into the seat as he came down hard on his side. Rising on a knee, he shot the man on Santor's right. In the next heartbeat he shot the man on Santor's left.

Jack Santor skipped backward, shooting as he went. He gained the hall and flew.

There was a sharp cry and a thump.

Fargo heaved upright and went after him. The butler was on the hall floor holding a hand to his bloody temple. Twenty feet beyond, Santor was going through a door. "Stay down," Fargo shouted, and snapped a shot. He missed.

The door opened into the kitchen. It was empty. Fargo flew into the night. A firefly blossomed. He answered and spied a figure bolting across the yard. His leg hardly pained him as he poured on speed.

Santor could run. He reached a fence and vaulted over it.

Fargo made for a different spot and did the same. He was in high grass, and crouched.

This part of the city was a mix of homes and land still in its wild state.

Fargo moved slowly. He made no sound but somehow Santor knew where he was; a shot stabbed the dark and a hornet buzzed.

Throwing himself flat, Fargo crawled until he came to some trees. Rising, he glided from cover to cover. He doubted Santor had run off. The gunman would want to end it. He crept around a pine. A log was in his way. He raised a leg to go over it and flame stabbed at him. Dropping behind it, he listened to the crash of brush.

Silence fell.

Fargo took off his hat and snaked around the log with it in his left hand. He was careful not to let his spurs jingle. He avoided spots where the vegetation was thickest. Minutes passed and he began to think he was wrong.

A black shape that Fargo took for a bush moved. He extended the Colt but he needed to be sure so he waited. The shape crept closer.

Jack Santor was bent at the knees and looking all around. Except at the ground in front of him.

Back the way they came shouts rose. Someone was yelling that William Mercer had been shot.

Fargo holstered the Colt, eased his right hand to his boot, and molded the toothpick to his fingers.

Santor had stopped to listen to the cries but now he was advancing again. His duster was open and a stray shaft of starlight glinted off his belt buckle.

Fargo waited until Santor was almost on top of him. Lunging up out of the grass, he grabbed Santor's wrist and at the same time thrust the toothpick to the hilt. Once, twice, and yet again, and Jack Santor collapsed with a groan. Fargo wrenched the ivory-handled Smith & Wesson from Santor's grasp and wedged it under his belt.

Santor was taking deep breaths. His lung had been punctured and he sounded like a blacksmith's bellows filled with water.

Fargo squatted. "All the trouble you went to, eh?"

"Bastard," Santor rasped.

"Who hired you?"

Santor let out a gurgling burst of air and blood. "It'll be a cold day in hell."

"You're done for." Fargo pointed out the obvious. "It can't make any difference."

"To you it will," Santor said weakly. "They'll kill the others and there's nothing you can do."

"Who will?"

Santor looked down at himself. "Always knew I'd die with my boots on but I never figured on it being a knife. You're good. If it hadn't been for you—" He stopped.

"Santor?" Fargo felt for a pulse in the killer's neck. "Damn." He went through Santor's pockets. In one was a poke. In another was a folded sheet of paper. He left the body there and returned to the house and on through it and out the front door.

A crowd had gathered and was talking excitedly. The butler was there, having his head nursed by a woman in an apron. All the talk ceased.

"Who are you, mister?" someone demanded. "What were you doing in there?"

Fargo went down the steps, amused at how they looked at him as they might a grizzly about to pounce.

"Didn't you hear him?" another man asked.

Fargo unwrapped the Ovaro's reins and reached for the saddle horn.

"You shouldn't go anywhere," a woman said. "The marshal is on his way. He'll want to talk to you, I bet."

Fargo's saddle creaked under him and he hooked the other stirrup. He reined around and the people parted. No one tried to stop him.

Once he was back on the main street he sought out a street lamp and drew rein next to it and dismounted.

The poke contained over five hundred dollars. The paper was stationery, and the name of the company was printed at the top. Names and addresses had been written down in a small, flowing hand—a woman's hand.

Fargo climbed back on the Ovaro. The Colorado Stage Company was up the street. The Cobb and Whitten Express was down it.

He reined down it.

Their office window glowed yellow. Otherwise all was quiet.

Fargo didn't knock. He opened the door and strode in.

Gil Whitten was at a desk, scribbling in an account book. He jumped and started to slide his hand under his jacket. "Oh!" he exclaimed. "It's you."

"Are you here alone?"

"Yes," Whitten said. "My partner and—" He got no further.

Miles Blackburn came through the back door with a revolver in his pudgy hand. "Greetings," he said cheerfully.

"Who the hell are you?" Whitten said.

Fargo almost went for his Colt. The hard jab of a gun against his spine dissuaded him. He looked over his shoulder, knowing who it was.

"Miss me?" Hitch said.

26

Fargo was relieved of his Colt, the Smith & Wesson, and the toothpick.

Hitch stepped back and set them on a chair. His face was swollen and split and black-and-blue from where Fargo beat him.

Miles Blackburn put his revolver to Gil Whitten's head and took Whitten's six-shooter and the cane and tossed them to the floor. "There now," he said.

Whitten regarded the pair and said, "What's the meaning of this? Is it a robbery?"

Blackburn grinned and winked at Fargo. "Not very smart, is he?"

"I'm not so sure I have it worked out myself," Fargo admitted.

"I'm disappointed," Blackburn said. "I thought that you, at least, would have."

"Enough gab," Hitch said. "Let's kill them and get on to the last one if they haven't done her already."

Fargo prepared to spring. It was suicide but he would be damned if he would die meekly.

"Ah, ah," Hitch said.

"Will one of you *please* tell me what this is about?" Gil Whitten virtually pleaded.

"No," Hitch said.

"Now, now." Blackburn sat on Whitten's desk. "Would you want to go to your grave not knowing?"

"Miles, damn it," Hitch said.

"Indulge me," Blackburn said. "I want to see the look on his face." He smiled at Whitten. "Someone tried to kill you, yes?"

Whitten nodded.

"And someone tried to kill William Mercer and Brandy Randall, too, yes?"

"Not her," Whitten said. "She only claimed someone did so no one would suspect her of wanting Mercer and Cobb and me dead."

"Ironic, isn't it, that she thought the same thing about you after Tangwaci bungled his attempts to kill her?"

"The stupid breed," Hitch said.

Whitten was still confused. "You and this Tangwaci were in cahoots, I take it?"

"Only in the sense that we were hired by the same person," Blackburn said. "Tangwaci Smith was to kill Brandy Randall and you. Jack Santor was to murder Mercer. And we, my dear man, were brought in only recently to deal with Mr. Fargo, there. Now you've been added to our list and here we are." He beamed and laughed. "Simple, yes?"

"Smith and Santor are dead," Fargo said.

"You killed them both? My goodness, you are formidable. Isn't he formidable, Mr. Hitch?"

"Miles," Hitch said.

"We're almost to it," Blackburn said. "Be patient."

"I thought Mercer was behind it," Fargo said. "The marshal told me that you knew him, and you were seen in his company."

"Mercer wanted to hire us as protectors, too, but he was too cheap to pay our fee." Blackburn chuckled. "Another irony for you. We were offered more by the person he wanted us to protect him from."

"Who is this person you keep talking about?" Whitten asked. "Who is behind it all?"

"Isn't it obvious?" Blackburn rejoined.

"There are two of them behind it," Fargo said.

"Excellent." Blackburn nodded. "You've finally pierced the veil, as it were. It's too late to save yourself, but congratulations."

"Honestly, Miles," Hitch said. "Let's get it over with. Someone could walk in at any moment."

"My impatient friend has a point." Blackburn stood. "But he is also forgetting something."

"I am not," Hitch said.

Miles Blackburn pointed his revolver at Fargo. "I want the money you took from us."

"Oh, that," Hitch said.

"It's in my poke."

"Give it to Mr. Hitch," Blackburn instructed. "No tricks, please."

Hitch held out his hand.

Fargo produced the poke. A flick of his finger, and the drawstring was loose. He started to hand it over and turned it upside down. Money spilled out, most of it bills but coins, too, and Hitch did what anyone would do—he glanced at the falling money.

Fargo leaped. Hitch instantly went to shoot and Fargo punched him in the throat. Behind him Blackburn's revolver thundered and there were curses and the sounds of a struggle. Hitch staggered, and Fargo punched him in the throat again. Something crunched. Gasping and wheezing, Hitch fell against a desk. He looked up in bewilderment as Fargo hit him a third time and then he was melting to the floor.

Snatching up his Colt from the chair, Fargo shot Hitch in the head and spun. Miles Blackburn was standing over Gil Whitten and about to shoot him. Fargo fired. So did Blackburn. Whitten cried out and went limp. Blackburn stared at the hole in his shirt and then at Fargo and said, "You truly are formidable." He folded to the floor.

Fargo went to Whitten. Empty eyes stared up at him. He shifted to Miles Blackburn, who, incredibly, was smiling.

"Well played, sir. And my associate, Mr. Hitch?"

Fargo shook his head.

"A pity. Well, on to whatever is after this life, if anything." Miles Blackburn coughed and died.

Fargo raced out and vaulted onto the Ovaro. Main Street was crowded but he didn't care. He rode like a madman.

A light was on in the Colorado Stage Company office. He hit the door with his shoulder and spilled inside but no one was there.

A light glowed in the stable and a crumpled form lay near it. It was Rafer, stabbed through the body. His fingers were dug into the dirt like claws.

Fargo ran inside and stopped. A rope with a noose had been thrown over a rafter and the noose placed around Brandy Randall's neck. She had been gagged and her hands and legs tied, and she was standing on a stool. Next to the stool, holding on to the other end of the rope, was Melissa Hart.

"Let go of that."

"I think not," Melissa said, and giggled.

Fargo had been careless. He felt a sharp sting in his back.

A man about Gil Whitten's age, nicely dressed, was holding a sword cane, the tip red with a drop of Fargo's blood.

"Tyree Cobb, I bet."

"None other," Cobb said, and gave a mock bow. "Drop the Colt."

Fargo complied. He would have been run through if he hadn't. "This was all your doing." He played for time. "You made Brandy and Gil think the other was out to get them so no one would suspect you when your hired killers took care of them both."

"A brilliant plan, don't you think?" Cobb said.

"Why Mercer? He put up money for Whitten and you to start your company."

"The greedy son of a bitch demanded forty percent of our profits in return," Cobb said. "I couldn't have that."

"Not when you wanted it all for yourself."

Melissa gave the rope a tug. "Quit dawdling, Tyree. Kill him and help me with her and it will finally be over. You'll be the stagecoach king and I'll have that fine house you promised and more money than I'll know what to do with."

"What was your part in this?" Fargo asked her. "Besides keeping an eye on me on that last run to Denver?"

"I helped him a lot," Melissa bragged. "We're in love," she said proudly, and smiled at Cobb. "He's going to take me for his wife."

"Even after you fucked me?"

"What was that?" Tyree Cobb said, and lowered the sword cane a little.

"Did you tell her to make love to me or did she do it on her own?" Fargo asked

Melissa didn't appear any too happy. "Don't listen to him, Tyree. I never did any such thing."

"I can prove it," Fargo said.

"Prove it how?" Cobb demanded.

Fargo remembered making love to her; he remembered how each time she said the same thing when she was caught up in the throes of passion. He reckoned that if she said it to him, she said it to others. He looked at Tyree Cobb and quoted her. "'Baby, give it to Momma.'"

Cobb lowered the sword cane even more. "You damn slut! I knew I shouldn't trust a saloon trollop. I just knew it."

"Don't, Tyree," Melissa said.

Fargo lunged and grabbed Cobb's sword arm even as he slugged the man in the face. The blow knocked Cobb back.

Fargo held on and swung again but Cobb ducked and arced a knee that caught Fargo close to where it would hurt the most. As it was, it caused him to stumble. That was all Cobb needed. Cobb wrenched, and his arm was free.

The sword flashed. Fargo sprang aside and the tip missed his neck. He tried to close but Cobb made a Z in the air and kept him at bay. Blood trickling from his mouth, Cobb began to circle.

"Clever bastard."

Fargo glanced right and left for something he could use to defend himself.

"Clever, clever bastard," Cobb said. "Everything was going smoothly and then you came along. But I won't let you stop me. With Brandy dead her company will fall apart. I'll buy it for a song and merge it with mine and have the only stage line between here and Denver."

"She's not dead yet." Fargo noticed a long, thin handle leaning against a stall.

"Thanks for reminding me." Cobb glanced at Melissa. "Finish her."

"Anything for you," Melissa said, and hauled on the rope.

Brandy gasped as her body arced into a bow. She was yanked onto her toes and lost her balance and slipped off the stool.

Fargo started toward her and had to jerk back when the sword slashed at his throat. Cobb smiled and attacked in earnest, thrusting and slashing. Cobb was good, and it was all Fargo could do to keep from suffering Rafer's fate. Turning, twisting, dodging, he retreated until he was only a step or two from the stall and the long handle.

Cobb hadn't seen it. He wagged the sword and said confidently, "You've gone as far as you can go."

Fargo risked a glance at Brandy. Melissa was straining at the rope and Brandy's face was a beet and she was desperately trying to take a breath.

Cobb stabbed at his chest.

Fargo sidestepped, felt a slight sting, and got hold of the long handle. Pivoting, he speared the pitchfork at a startled Cobb, who bounded out of reach and blurted, "What the hell?"

Fargo went after him. He lanced the tines at Cobb's face and Cobb parried with the sword. He thrust low and Cobb parried again, and grinned.

"I am a master swordsman, fool."

"That's nice," Fargo said. He thrust low again and Cobb swept the sword low to counter it but it was a feint. Fargo had thrust low but he went high. The tines sheared into Tyree Cobb's chest like hot knives into butter. Cobb shrieked as he was impaled. Fargo wrenched the pitchfork out and drove it in again, lower down. Cobb screeched. Then Cobb was collapsing and Fargo heard a rush of footsteps and he tore the pitchfork out and spun.

Melissa was almost on him. She had a knife raised and was about to stab him in the back. She ran straight into the pitchfork and jolted to a stop and said, "Oh God."

Fargo let go and ran to Brandy. She was on the floor, still struggling. He tore at the rope and when he couldn't loosen the noose fast enough he quickly drew his toothpick and cut it. She uttered a strangled cry and sucked in air and he cradled her head in his lap as she went on sucking until she could breathe again.

Brandy looked up with tears in her eyes. "Thank you," she said softly, and suddenly her eyes widened.

Fargo jerked his head up.

Melissa was still alive. She had pulled the pitchfork out and held it in both hands and was about to bury it in him.

There was a shot, just one, and the top of her head exploded. Without a sound she pitched to the ground, convulsed, and was gone.

Marshal Shicklin came down the aisle. He stared at Melissa and then at Tyree Cobb and said, "So it was them all along. I suspected as much."

"And you didn't arrest them?"

"I needed proof." Shicklin nudged Melissa with his toe and chuckled. "See? I'm not totally worthless."

Fargo slid his arms under Brandy and lifted her and started for the door.

"Where are you going?" Marshal Shicklin asked.

"Away from you," Skye Fargo said and carried Brandy out into the cool of the night.

LOOKING FORWARD!
The following is the opening
section of the next novel in the exciting
***Trailsman* series from Signet:**

TRAILSMAN #358
SIX-GUN VENDETTA

Santa Fe, New Mexico Territory, 1860—
where four murdering curs learn the hard way
what the word "friend" means to Skye Fargo.

"C'mon out, old-timer!" shouted a thickset man hiding behind a mesquite tree. "We ain't desperadoes, just prospectors down on our luck! All we ask is a spot of grub."

"Prospectors! That's a hoot," retorted a tired and gravelly voice from inside the weather-beaten shack. "Ain't no color nowheres near here. And I've seed enough skunk-bit coyotes in my day. You aim to murder me, so let's get thrashing."

"Aww, hell, old roadster," Baylis Ulrick tried again. "This ain't Christian of you. My throat is parched and my backbone is scraping against my ribs."

"Happens you was just hungry men down on their luck," the old man shouted back, "you'da just walked up and give me the hail. But I seen the four of you sneaking up on the place like warpath Comanches, clubs to hand. You've busted loose from a hoosegow someplace, and you mean to rob and kill me."

Ulrick was a big, heavy-jowled, flint-eyed man in home-spun shirt and trousers and a rawhide vest. Like his companions hidden nearby in an erosion ditch, he was filthy and unshaven, his clothing sorely used. He gave the high sign to a hatchet-profiled man in the ditch. The man nodded and felt the sandy ground for a good rock.

"All right, we was locked up in Chimayo," Ulrick said, eyeing the shack's leather-hinged door. "We locked horns with some Mexers and got jugged for disturbing the peace."

"That's a neat trick seeing's how there ain't no sheriff *nor* jail in Chimayo. Not too many Mexers neither—'bout what you might expect in an Indian village."

The hatchet-profiled man had found a couple of rocks and was trotting down the ditch, trying to get wide of the view from the shack's only window. The other two men twigged the game and headed in the opposite direction. The old salt was well armed and a good shot.

"Listen, Pop, nobody out west tells the truth. That don't make everybody killers. My hand to God, all we ask is a sup of water. We're all dry as a year-old cow chip. I give you my word we won't try a fox play."

"Your word don't mean spit. Now move on from here or my next shot won't be a warning."

Ulrick had a hair-trigger temper and it suddenly laid a red film over his vision. His breathing quickened until it whistled in his nostrils.

"If we're such hard cases," he shouted in a new tone of impatience, "how's come we ain't boosted that fine horse-flesh in your corral? Ain't no window in the back of your shack, we coulda just rode out with 'em."

"Oh, you figger to do that, all right. But you need guns and food, too, and that means killing me. So let's just open the ball."

"Make you a deal, you old pus-gut. If you light out right now, we'll let you live. Otherwise, you'll die hard and I guar-andamntee it."

"I got a better idea," the old man shot back. "Why'n'cha stick your dick in your ear and make a jug handle out of it?"

Immediately after this suggestion, his rifle spoke its piece. Baylis flinched hard when the slug raised a yellow plume of dust close to his exposed left foot. His eyes turned smoky with rage. Neither he nor the three men with him had a sulfur match between them, or they could have just burned the old rooster out.

Baylis glanced to his right and saw that Jed was in place. On his left, Hiram and Ray were almost set.

"All right, old man," he muttered, his tone heavy with menace. "It's time to fish or cut bait."

Despite his tough talk, Corey Webster tasted the corroded-pennies taste of fear.

Over his long life he had survived his share of scrapes. A man couldn't trap beaver with the likes of Caleb Green and Jim Bridger in the heyday of the Shining Times without sleeping on his weapons and shooting plumb every time. Corey had fought savages in the Stony Mountains before the U.S. Army even knew how to get there. And long before Skye Fargo became the famous Trailsman, Corey had helped to scrape the green off the kid's antlers.

But this today was dangerously different. In his mountain-man days the skirmishes were usually in the open, where a man could see around him and duck for cover. Now he was trapped in a clapboard box, and despite a bevy of good firearms he had foolishly run low on black powder and cartridges.

All these thoughts skittered around inside his head like frenzied rodents, but the old trapper was steady and determined, even fierce-eyed. Even his wooden leg had not banked his fires over the years.

He knew he was trapped between the sap and the bark. He could never manage to get horsed before this pack of mad dogs would bring him to ground. But without ammo, neither could he continue to hold them off from inside the shack.

Keeping his head sideways, Corey glanced out the window into the glaring sunshine. The big mouthpiece in the rawhide vest was still holed up behind the mesquite tree—he could see part of his left leg. But Corey knew he could no longer afford potshots. He was determined to plug at least one of these jackals before they sent him to glory.

His hands clutched a .44-caliber North & Savage rifle. He had traded some red-fox furs for it in Santa Fe, realizing it would be a superb repeating weapon for scrapes just like this one. But Montezuma's revenge had given him a bad case of the trots and laid him up before he could stock up on loads.

He clicked the cylinder around—one shot left.

"Place is a goddamn armory," he upbraided himself, "and all worthless. How many times did I tell Fargo a weapon without loads is like water without the wet?"

Corey had pulled a battered deal table in front of the door and piled his weapons on it. An old Kentucky over-and-under, a good gun, lay useless for lack of primer caps. Likewise with his four-barrel shotgun—each barrel had its own frizzen and pan, but he had no powder to pour into them.

"Where's them other three sons a bitches?" Corey wondered aloud. He could no longer spot them peeking at the shack. Flanking the place, most likely, he realized.

"My offer is still good, old man," the mouthpiece shouted. "Light a shuck out of there now and you'll be gumming your supper tonight."

"Gum a cat's tail, you murderin' graveyard rat!"

A piece of foolscap on the table caught Corey's eye. He picked it up and read it.

Corey, I hope the courier delivers this before I arrive in New Mexico Territory. The army is paying me rich man's wages to lead a mapmaking detail into the Sangre de Cristo range. But if you're still alive, you tough old grizz, I plan to visit you first. The army can wait.

Skye

"If I'm still alive," Corey repeated. "All hell's a-poppin', Skye. Ride in now, boy, and give this shit-eating trash a lead bath."

They were the last words ever spoken by Corey Webster. He glimpsed sudden movement to the left of the window and swung his rifle in that direction. An eyeblink later a tall, skinny man jumped in from the right, a classic diversion. His right arm was already cocked and released a fist-sized rock at Corey almost point-blank. Force like a mule kick made the old man stagger back as an orange starburst exploded inside his skull.

He folded like an empty sack, the rifle dropping to the rammed-earth floor beside him. A cheer erupted from without.

"Nice work, Jed," Baylis Ulrick called out as he ran toward the shack. "You brained the old bastard good."

The four men struggled for a moment to open the blocked door, then crowded into the one-room shack. Hiram Steele, a small, hard-knit man with furtive eyes and a pockmarked face, knelt beside the old-timer.

"Christ on a crutch!" he exclaimed. "Half his forehead is crushed in like an eggshell, but the old goat is still breathing!"

Ulrick's eyes flicked toward the bowie knife on the table. "Not for long he ain't, chappies."

Hearing this, the other three men exchanged silent glances. Ulrick, with his hard-hitting fists and take-charge manner, was a natural-born leader of desperate men. But before he took to the owlhoot trail he had been trained as a butcher in Chicago. As they had recently learned, he had not completely left his old trade behind.

"Wood ticks in my Johnny!" exclaimed a man with green-rimmed teeth and gums the color of raw liver. Ray Nearhood pointed to a shelf made of crossed sticks. It held modest but welcome provisions: a cheesecloth sack filled with jerked beef, cans of coffee and sugar, a sack of cornmeal.

"And glom the weapons the old cheese dick had," Jed Longstreet marveled, picking up the heavy but dangerous-looking flintlock shotgun. "This thing's a relic but, by hell, it's got four barrels! You rotate 'em by hand."

He did so, and all four men were impressed at the sharp, precise clicks as each barrel snapped into place. The vintage weapon was in mint condition.

"I seen them hand cannons in the Mexican War," Baylis explained. "A man could toss a biscuit farther than that piece shoots. But close up, one shot will strip the clothes off three men standing shoulder to shoulder. It's heavy, but we'll pack it along. Might come in handy."

Hiram Steele picked up the North & Savage. "Thissen's old, too, but it's a repeater. The trigger guard is combined with the lever, see? When you move it you revolve the cylinder and cock the hammer."

"It's big bore so we'll take it," Ulrick decided. "Piss on that Kentucky rifle. We'll get more guns someplace. See any ammo?"

As the men looked around, Longstreet spotted the letter under the table. He swooped down to pick it up. "Any of you boys know how to read?"

Ulrick snatched it from his hand and read it aloud.

"Katy Christ!" Nearhood erupted when Baylis read the signature. "This old fartsack was chums with the Trailsman?"

"Who's this Trailsman?" demanded Hiram, busy tossing the provisions into a gunny sack.

"Where you been grazing?" Nearhood replied. "They say he's the toughest hombre ever born of woman."

"The Trailsman," Longstreet chimed in. "Well, carry me out. Carry me out with tongs! They claim he can track an ant across rocks."

"That's bad news," Ulrick sneered, "for ants."

"Ray ain't birding," Longstreet assured him. "I hear Fargo is six sorts of trouble. And if he's coming to visit this old geezer, they must be chummy. Baylis, maybe you oughtn't to . . . you know, carve him up like you done them guards in the Manzanas."

Ulrick's big, bluff features twisted into a mask of contempt. "Shit, listen to the ladies' sewing circle! You boys believe too much barroom josh. Anyhow, you know how it is with travel time out here. Fargo could be a month off still. Ain't no witnesses saw us, so how will the big bad Trailsman even know who to trail?"

"That rings right," Nearhood agreed. "'Sides, Apaches,

Kiowa, and Comanches raid in these parts. The way Baylis sets to work, it looks like wild Indians done it."

Ulrick nodded. "That's the gait. You boys round up whatever tack you can and get them horses ready to raise dust."

He picked up the bowie knife from the table and tested its edge with a finger. "Not bad. I wish I had me a boning knife and a cleaver, too, but this is all right for rough-gutting."

"I don't like it," Longstreet objected again. "It's bad enough that Fargo will find his old pal cold as a wagon wheel. Why poke fire with a sword by butchering him out?"

Baylis squatted, stiff kneecaps popping. "Finding his chum with a crushed skull will surely raise Fargo's ire. But finding him with his entrails stacked on his chest just might scare the fight out of him."

"Maybe," Longstreet said as he went out the door. "But that ain't what I hear."

No other series packs this much heat!

THE TRAILSMAN

"A writer in the tradition of Louis L'Amour
and Zane Grey!"

—*Huntsville Times*

National Bestselling Author

RALPH COMPTON

**Available wherever books are sold or at
penguin.com**